P9-BYJ-585

Snail Mail No More

Snail Mail No More

Paula Danziger
& Ann M. Martin

Shepherd Middle School
Ottawa, Illinois 61350

SCHOLASTIC INC.

New York   Toronto   London   Auckland   Sydney
Mexico City   New Delhi   Hong Kong   Buenos Aires

If you purchased this book without a cover, you should be aware
that this book is stolen property. It was reported as "unsold and destroyed"
to the publisher, and neither the author nor the publisher
has received any payment for this "stripped book."

No part of this publication may be reproduced, stored in a retrieval system,
or transmitted in any form or by any means, electronic, mechanical,
photocopying, recording, or otherwise, without written permission
of the publisher. For information regarding permission, write to
Scholastic Inc., Attention: Permissions Department,
557 Broadway, New York, NY 10012.

ISBN-13: 978-0-439-06336-4
ISBN-10: 0-439-06336-1

Copyright © 2000 by Paula Danziger. Copyright © 2000 by Ann M. Martin.
All rights reserved. Published by Scholastic Inc.
SCHOLASTIC, APPLE PAPERBACKS, and associated logos are
trademarks and/or registered trademarks of Scholastic Inc.

12 11 10 9 8 7 6 5 4 3   8 9 10 11 12 13/0

Printed in the U.S.A.   40

First Scholastic paperback printing, September 2000

Text type was set in Verdana and Skia. Display type was set in Greymantle.
Book design by Marijka Kostiw

To the three wonderful editors who guided
Tara★Starr, Elizabeth, and us:
Craig Walker, Liz Szabla, and Brenda Bowen.

—P.D. & A.M.M.

Snail Mail
No More

Elizabeth

June 25

Dear Tara★Starr,

I just got your letter! I didn't wait a single second to answer it. It's lying here on my desk. I read it for the first
time a minute or so ago, then I read it about twenty
more times, and now I'm writing back to you. Oh, I
can't wait for Mom to come home from work so I can
ask her when I can visit you. Just think, Tara, a whole
week together. I figure it's been 44 weeks since we saw
each other. Do you think we can make up for that in
one week? I do. (Maybe.)

Oh, I am so excited. About our visit, of course,
PLUS . . . school's out!

Also, I have to admit that I'm thrilled to say good-bye
to seventh grade. It's been a year of so many changes,

most of them difficult. You moved away, Dad started drinking, Dad lost his job, we lost our house, Dad left us, we moved here to the apartment at DEER RUN. Actually, some good things have happened too. Even though I don't like the apartment itself, I like living in DEER RUN. Remember how I made fun of that name at first? I still think it's a dumb name, but I like the complex. And I like living near Howie and Susie. I'm so glad we've become good friends.

Speaking of Howie and Susie, guess what we're going to be able to do this summer. Send e-mail. Can you believe it? Mom's bringing an old computer home from her office (I think she's bringing it <u>today</u>), and Susie's going to set it up so that I can have e-mail. I've already chosen my e-mail name. It's Eliz812 — part of my name, and my birthday. What do you think?

Oh, boy. I'm just stalling for time until Mom comes home. I really can't wait to ask her about our visit, but there's no point in calling her at work because she won't be able to concentrate on a nonwork matter. Also, she won't have the right calendar with her.

You know what, Tara? I think I'm going to go ahead and mail this letter, because walking it to the mailbox

will be a little activity. Then I'll write you another letter tonight after Mom and I have talked.

More soon.

I love you.

And I am SO EXCITED!!!!!!!!!!!!!

Love,

Elizabeth

Elizabeth

Dear Tara★Starr,

Mom and I just got finished talking, and guess what. Mom thinks early July would be a good time for me to visit you. Isn't that great? It's almost July NOW!!! We could be together in just one week! Mom is going to look into a couple of things at her office, and I'm going to talk to Susie to find out if early July would be okay for her to take over my job of watching Emma while Mom's at work. Then Mom is going to call you guys tomorrow night. So by the time you get this letter (and the one I wrote this afternoon), we'll probably have the trip pretty much worked out. (Which makes this letter kind of silly, doesn't it? Oh, well.)

I'm too excited to end this letter here. I have diarrhea of the pen. I really wish you had a computer so we could send each other e-mail too. Then we could practically TALK to each other with the computers, instead of having to wait three or four days for our letters to be delivered via snail mail. With e-mail we could write to each other several times a day. We could tell each other everything that happens, practically AS it happens. For instance, right now I could tell you what I just made for supper. With e-mail that would be interesting because you could read about it this very evening. With snail mail you won't read about it until three days after the meal, so who cares?

Speaking of supper, after supper tomorrow night Howie and Susie and I are going to ride our bikes to the Dair-E Freez and treat ourselves to sundaes. I'll get rainbow sprinkles in your honor.

Love,

Elizabeth

Dear Elizabeth,

I am soooooooooooooooooooooooooooo excited.

Please, oh please, oh please . . . get here as soon as you can.

It'll be so great to see you.

It's weird . . . ten whole months without seeing you. I know a lot about your life from your letters. (The ones you sent and the ones you DIDN'T send. . . . Remember our fight?????!!!!!!!) I know about your feelings. Well, a lot about your feelings. I know you keep a lot to yourself too. What I don't know is what you look like. Did you get taller? (I did . . . four inches.) Did your bust get any bigger? (My bra size has gone from an A to a B. . . . I'm glad we're talking lingerie, not grades!) Is your hair long or short? Is it the same color? (Mine is back to normal except for a violet streak in the front.) I know you'll be here soon and I can see for myself . . . but I am soooooooooo impatient.

Elizabeth, I just reread the paragraph before this one and realize how many times I said, "I know." Does that make me a know-it-all? DON'T ANSWER THAT!!!!!!

Anyway, I just can't wait until you get here.

Barb and Luke and I will meet you at the airport and then we'll take you back to the apartment, where you can rest for the evening. The next day, the festivities begin. Some of my friends will come over and we can all shop. That night, we'll have a PARTY and invite over a bunch of my friends. It'll be a party in your honor. (When I told Barb about this, she said I should check it out with you . . . that all that attention might not be something you'd love. But I can't believe you wouldn't want to do this. I mean, I know you are shy, but you can do this. . . . Just think of how much fun it's going to be.)

And don't worry about where you are going to sleep. Luke and Barb went to a house sale last weekend and bought a trundle bed for my room. It was really cheap. <u>And</u> it means I have room for a friend to stay over whenever I want. The couple was selling a lot of stuff because they're retiring.

It was weird. Even though the people who were selling all the stuff are old, they got along really well with my parents, who, as you know, are not even thirty yet. And as Luke said, not very retiring folks. Ho-ho. Ha-ha. The Coopers thought it was "cute" that I was an almost-thirteen-year-old only child who was soon not going to be an only child. So they also sold us things that their grandchildren no longer need, like a crib, a high chair, and a car seat!!!!! I really don't want to talk about that right now . . . and when you come here, even though I am getting better about it, I don't want to deal with the B-word. (As in B-aby.) Anyway, I have the trundle bed so that's good.

Please, oh please let me know exactly when you are going to be here.

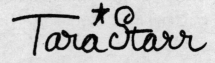

P.S. About the name for your e-mail address. It's so YOU!!!

Elizabeth

Dear Tara★Starr

I'm answering your letter even though my mom and your mom are going to talk again tonight to finalize our plans. I know this is going to happen because Mom just called me from her office and said that Barb had called <u>her</u> to talk about our visit, and they arranged that Mom would phone Barb tonight when both of them will really be able to talk.

You asked what I look like. I don't think I look any different than when you left last fall, but I guess I must have changed. Wait — maybe I'll go measure myself.

Okay, I'm back. And I'm five feet, two inches tall now, but I just realized I don't know how tall I was at the beginning of the school year. I must have grown, though. I had to get almost all new summer clothes last month because I couldn't fit into any of last year's. (Mom saved the old ones for Emma. Poor thing. They won't fit her for about seven years. What a dork she'll look like then.) Even though I grew, I'm the same weight I was last summer. I know that for sure. Mom says I look wispy. Susie says I'm a beanpole. My hair is about the same length and it's the exact same color. I have bangs now, though, so that's a little difference.

Tara, I want to say one thing about the party. I love the idea of having a party to meet your friends, but can it just be a plain old party? Not one in my honor? Barb's right — I don't want all that attention. But I'd like to meet your friends. And a party sounds like fun. (It isn't going to be a kissing party, though, is it? I don't think I'm ready for that. I haven't been to one of those, and the first time I do go to one, I'd like to be with kids I already know. Well, actually, I'd particularly like to be with Howie.)

I think it's great that you and Barb and Luke got all that stuff at a house sale. We've seen a lot of sales around here so far this summer, and Mom got Emma a little tiny bicycle with training wheels at one. It's in really good shape and only cost $15. The ones we were looking at in Toys 'Я' Us cost WAY more than that. Mom also got me a new bedspread, since mine had been ripped in the move. I think house sales are the only way to go when you're on a budget.

The Fourth of July is in two days and guess what. Howie and Susie and I are going to go to the fireworks display at the park. We're going to go by ourselves and get dinner there and everything. Remember when we went last year? And you could buy food from those trucks? Well, I've been saving the $$ Mom has been paying me to take care of Emma this summer, and I know exactly what I'm going to buy for dinner: a hot dog with everything, French fries, and a vanilla ice-cream cone with sprinkles (although I wonder if an ice-cream cone is too messy to eat in front of Howie).

I could go on and on, Tara, but I'm going to stop for two reasons: 1. I have to go get dinner ready. 2. I'm sure I'm going to be talking to you in a couple of hours.

And I KNOW I'm going to see you VERY SOON!!!

Lots of Love,

Elizabeth

P.S. Bust? What bust?

July 6

Dear Elizabeth,

I CAN'T BELIEVE IT!!

It's finally happening. After our letters, our phone calls, our mothers' phone calls . . . we're finally going to see each other. Only one more week to go. I can hardly wait!!!!!!!!!!

We're going to have the most wonderful time.

AND I HAVE THE MOST WONDERFUL NEWS!!!!!!!!!!!!!

GUESS WHAT????????????????????????????????????

Darn . . . it's so hard to play "guess what" in letters. It will be so much easier in person. I'll just have to tell you WHAT!!!!!!!!!!

The Lane Family . . . Luke and Barb and TARA . . . are getting a computer. A COMPUTER . . . and what's more, WE ARE GETTING E-MAIL! That's right, Elizabeth. . . . SNAIL MAIL NO MORE!

I am soooooooooooooooooooooooooooooooo happy. We will be able to send each other e-mail ALL THE TIME. And this really cute guy even explained to me that we'll be able to send each other instant messages (I don't know how that works, but he said that he would teach me how to do IMs. Is that anything like BMs???? I know . . . I'm being gross. Sorry.) Anyway, I'll be able to e-mail you, Eliz812. I wonder what my e-mail address will be?????? Tara★ . . . or TARA★LANE . . . or maybe just ★ . . . We'll have to discuss that when you get here.

I bet you're surprised that we're getting a computer!!!!! Remember the Cooper family???? They decided to get a new computer and sell their old one to us. Well, not even sell it to us. Luke and Barb and I are going to "work" for it . . . help them pack up for the move. We would have done that for them anyway. (They are soooooo nice.)

So now we can talk on e-mail. I was jealous that you and what's-their-faces (OK . . . I know their names are Howie and Susie) could e-mail each other, even if you do live in the same town, in fact in the same apartment complex, and are always going for ice cream together!

I know . . . I am glad that you are friends with them . . . but I am just a <u>little worried</u>. I hope that you don't like them more than you like me. And speaking of that, there is something that I have to tell you. I am afraid that you are going to like my new friends more than you like me . . . and that they are going to like you more than they like me. So I was thinking of telling everyone that it was OK for everyone to like each other, just not more than me.

Well, I guess that's it for now.

Elizabeth, think about it! There's just enough time for you to get this letter . . . and then the next time we are in contact . . . it will actually be FACE-TO-FACE.

I can't wait.

Love,

Tara*Starr

Date: July 14 10:49:58 AM
From: TSTARR
Subj: Snail Mail No More
To: Eliz812

DEAR ELIZABETH,

GUESS WHAT . . . TARA★STARR LANE HAS E-MAIL!!
AND THIS IS MY FIRST E-MAIL THAT I HAVE EVER
SENT. . . . And I am sending it to you, my friend Elizabeth, who is actually sitting right here next to me,
teaching me how to do this.

We have worked it out so that we can each get and
send our own e-mail from my computer while you are
here . . . and what's more, it's PRIVATE, with our own
secret passwords and everything.

I AM SO EXCITED. . . . THIS IS SO WONDERFUL. . . .
BUT WHAT IS EVEN MORE WONDERFUL THAN DO-
ING THIS IS THE FACT THAT YOU, ELIZABETH, ARE
FINALLY ACTUALLY HERE WITH ME AND WE'RE
HAVING THE BEST BEST BEST TIME . . . AND IT'S
ONLY JUST BEGINNING.

Please e-mail me back right now so that we know this
actually works, and then we can go have ice-cream
cones with sprinkles!!!!!!!!!!!!!!!!!!!!!!!!

Love,
Tara★Starr

Date: July 14 10:54:09 AM
From: Eliz812
Subj: Ice Cream
To: TSTARR

Dear Tara,

It worked! I got into my account and found your letter (as you know). Now go away. Don't sit here beside me while I write to you.

Thank you. (Won't you have more fun reading your mail if you haven't watched me write your letter?)

Tara, being here with you is so cool!!! I love it. I love seeing Barb and Luke and Barb's stomach — my first introduction to the baby. (Do you mind my saying that?)

The real purpose of this letter is to find out about the ice cream. Are we going to have ice cream for lunch? Where is your ice-cream place? Does it have rainbow sprinkles? A flavor of the month?

Okay, enough of this letter writing. Let's go!

Love,
Elizabeth

Date: July 15 9:22:31 AM
From: TSTARR
Subj: YOU ARE HERE
To: Eliz812

DEAR ELIZABETH,
I KNOW. I KNOW. ALL CAPITAL LETTERS MEAN I'M
SHOUTING. BUT I JUST CAN'T HELP MYSELF. YOU
ARE HERE. . . . YOU ARE ACTUALLY HERE IN OHIO.

ALL RIGHT. I'll calm down. You are here. . . . You are
actually here.

I am soooooooooooo happy.

I have a lot of new friends here, but none of them knows
me the way you do . . . knows what it used to be like before my parents decided to act (be) more grown-up,
more responsible . . . how hard it was when they didn't

have regular steady jobs. None of them knows that sometimes I'm not as sure of myself as I pretend to be.

And there is no one here I know as well as I know you.

I am soooooooooooo glad you are here.

SO GLAD. . . . Okay, I'll calm down again. I know you like things quieter than I sometimes do.

I can't wait for you and Barb to get back from the store. I know you both said you just wanted to make a "donut run" (I hope you get lots of the ones with rainbow sprinkles!!!!!). But I know you two really just want to be alone to talk. That's okay. I'm only a little jealous. I know you and my mother have always had your "private chats." And I know that without me along you will be able to gush about the BTB. (That's Baby To Be. Isn't BTB much better than when I was calling IT the DS — Demon Seed?!?!)

I forgot how early you wake up. I know you tried to be very quiet . . . but 6 AM. I can't believe you were up and sewing at that hour!!! And I do think it is very sweet of you to be making something for the baby, my future brother or sister. I'm sorry I asked you if the bottom part will be big enough for cloven hooves. (I guess I've watched too many horror movies . . . which I know you hate. Remember the time we saw *Rosemary's Baby* and you practically passed out?!)

Anyway, today we'll go sightseeing. I'll show you my school. (It's sooo much bigger than our old one. Well, my old one . . . you are still there.) And we can walk past Darren Ross's house. He's sooooo nice. All the girls like him. You'll meet him at the party tomorrow night. And we can go hang out at the mall for a while. They have a big fabric store there. I bet you'll really like it. I can go into the crafts section and look for things for making jewelry. It'll be just like "old times." (It's funny to think about old times when we're just kids . . . but growing-up kids.)

Well, that's it for now. You and Barb'll be back any sec. I just wanted to practice on the computer and send you this e-mail to say I'M GLAD YOU ARE HERE.

Your excited friend,
Tara★Starr

Date: July 15 4:14:55 PM
From: Eliz812
Subj: Extreme Nervousness
To: Mouse16

Dear Susie,

Hi! How is everything going? How is Emma doing? Is she behaving herself? Will you ever baby-sit for her again? Tell her that her big sister misses her very much and give her this message: Sylvester Mc-Monkey McBean. I can't tell you what it means, but Emma will know. It's part of our secret code.

I'm having a great time seeing Tara again. Susie, she lives in the nicest apartment. It's really cool. It's in an old house. Barb and Luke are just like I remember them, except that they have real jobs and are SO much more organized. And of course Barb is pregnant, so she looks different, at least from the side.

Tara and I have been sightseeing (Tara's word). There aren't really any sights here, not like monuments or something. The sights are Tara's school, the ice-cream place (flavor-of-the-month: Berry Blast, which is red, white, and blue), the mall (which has an EXCELLENT sewing store), Barb's office, Luke's office, the hospital where the baby will be born, the school where Barb and Luke are getting their college degrees, Tara's favorite jewelry store, and stuff like that. I love seeing Tara's world. I'll be able to picture Tara in it when I write to her from now on.

Confession: I am getting SO nervous. Tonight is the night of the party Tara planned, the one I told you about before I left. I talked her out of having it in my honor, but she's still having it. ALL her friends are going to be there. It's, like, 15 kids. And one of them is Darren Ross, this kid she has a huge crush on. I think she met him when he helped set up her computer. I'm a little hazy on the details. All I know is that he's cute, nice, all the girls like him, and Tara has invited him to the party. I think she's hoping to get to know him better tonight. Susie, I hope I don't do anything to embarrass Tara in front of her friends. I just hate parties. I never know what to say to people, especially ones I haven't met before. Also, I can't figure out what to wear. Whatever I choose is probably going to be way too plain, but I don't have anything else. And no money to get anything else. And even if I did have $$, there's not enough time to go shopping. The party starts in just a few hours.

Pray for me.

Anxious in Ohio,
Elizabeth XXOO

Date: July 15 5:05:21 PM
From: TSTARR
Subj: I am getting nervous!!!!!!!!!!!!!!!!!!!!!!!!!!!!!!!
To: Palindrome

Dear Hannah,

I am getting soooooooooo nervous . . . but I don't want Elizabeth to find out that I am getting soooooooooo nervous. That's why I'm not calling you to talk. (What if Elizabeth accidentally overheard the call?) She's right in the next room with Luke. (I'm loaning her my father since . . . oh, well. Never mind. It's a long story and it's her story, so I don't want to say anything.) Anyway, they are in the kitchen talking. She's showing him the poetry journal she's editor of.

I'm nervous about the party . . . and about THE SECRET PLAN. I really hope Elizabeth and Darren like each other so we can all triple date. (How could Jeff's parents have decided to go to Disneyland this week???? Don't they have any respect for my plans??!!?? After he promised to take Elizabeth out!!!!) But never mind. On to Plan B. I really think Elizabeth and Darren will get along. After all, they are both kind of quiet . . . and really nice.

I love our plan for the triple date. We go to Mickey D's for dinner and then we go to the new place for miniature golf. Perfecto.

Let's just hope this works out. It'll be soooo much fun. I'm going to be positive about this. . . . I know Elizabeth and Darren are going to ADORE each other.

And remember, just because Elizabeth is visiting doesn't mean you are not my Ohio best friend. . . . YOU ARE!!!!!!!!!!!

Your Ohio best friend,
Tara ★ Starr

Date: July 16 12:41:38 AM
From: Eliz812
Subj: Party
To: Mouse16

Dear Susie,

This is a VERY quick note. Party is over. Just told Tara I was going to go brush my teeth, then ran out here to the computer to give you an update.

I think the party went well. I had fun. Am confused, though. Tara introduced me to Darren, that guy she thinks is so cute, but then she spent entire evening with Bart, old boyfriend. What's going on? Thought Tara wanted to get together with new guy.

Anyway, did not embarrass myself or Tara at any time during party. Was nice and polite and not geeky with cute Darren. (Howie's cuter.) And LOVED Hannah, who's one of Tara's best friends here. Hannah and I spent almost the whole evening talking.

Okay. Better go. More tomorrow.

Love,
Elizabeth

Date: July 16 10:22:45 AM
From: TSTARR
Subj: Farts
To: Palindrome

Hannah, my pal,
This is sooooooooooo funny. I wish you'd been at breakfast this morning to hear what happened.

After the MAJOR cleanup, Elizabeth and I were sitting around (she was eating the granola cereal I bought especially for her, and I was eating my Chocobits cereal) and we were talking. She said that she had a great time at the party and that her favorite person was YOU . . . that she's glad you and I are such close friends, that we all have "excellent" taste in friends. I agree, don't you? (I just knew the two of you would like each other . . . although not more than me, right?????)

Anyway, I asked her, "So what do you think of Darren? Isn't he nice?"

And Elizabeth said, "Yes, but I'm confused. I thought you had a crush on him, and then you spent the whole party with Bart."

I started to laugh and explained to her that I wanted her and Darren to like each other and triple date with us. Elizabeth, in her very calm Elizabeth way, said, "Well, if that's what you wanted, why didn't you tell me?"

Good point.

Anyway, it turns out that she's got this gigantic crush on a guy back home named Howie but doesn't know how to let him know . . . isn't even sure she wants to let him know.

I think that before she goes back, we've got to give her lessons on how to deal with boys.

Anyway, we ended up laughing a lot about it.

Oh, thanks for sending me the e-mail about July being "Bean Appreciation Month" with the fart sounds on it.

It's incredibly gross. I'm going to play it for Elizabeth after I e-mail this.

Anyway, back to the triple-date thing. Elizabeth and I decided that it should be a double-and-a-half date . . . that the five of us can go out and have a great time.

Gotta go. Luke is going to take Elizabeth and me to the mall. She needs to pick up some more buttons for the baby thing she's sewing for my Future Sibling.

Talk to you later.

Love,
Tara★Starr

P.S. I know what *your* name spells backwards . . . I just figured out that *my* name backwards (without the extra r) is Rats A Rat. . . . Gross.

Date: July 17 10:35:21 AM
From: Eliz812
Subj: Father
To: Mouse16

Dear Susie,

Have you heard the news yet? Have you talked to Mom? Well, she probably wouldn't have told you, but Emma might have said something. She was the one who broke the news to me.

This is SUCH bad news, Susie.

Dad is back. I mean, he called. He hasn't been in touch with us in weeks. I really thought he was gone forever. I wish he WERE gone forever. I like it so much better when he's out of our lives.

This is how I found out: Last night Mom and Emma called for a quick chat. I was SO glad to hear their voices. Mom and I talked first and I told her about the party and sightseeing and everything. Then Emma wanted to say hi, but the second Mom handed the phone to her she said, "Elizabeth, Daddy called and Mommy cried."

Well, Mom was back on the phone in a flash. "Honey," she said, "I was going to wait until you came home to tell you. I didn't want to spoil your vacation."

I said, "So he really did call?"

"Yes. The night before last."

"Why did you cry?"

Mom paused. "Because he was drunk."

Suddenly I didn't have any more questions, so Mom and I ended the conversation.

Isn't that awful, Susie?

Why did Dad have to resurface? I wish he would just go someplace far away and never bother us again. He's ruining everything.

Love,
Elizabeth

Date: July 18 12:08:52 PM
From: TSTARR
Subj: Double-and-a-half date . . . what fun!
To: Eliz812

OK. So I got the low score in miniature golf. Well, actually the high score . . . 198. So what if everyone else managed to have scores of less than 100?

Hi, Elizabeth . . . I know it's a little silly to send you an e-mail while you are still here, in fact in the kitchen once more talking with my mom about my Future Sibling. (Maybe after it's born I'll send it to you so you can be its big sister. OK, just kidding. I know you don't have room for it . . . and I'll try to stop calling it IT.)

Anyway, I'm sending this to you for two reasons:

   1. I'm still practicing how to send e-mails.

2. There's a lot I want to say that's easier to say this way instead of in person, but once you read all of this, we can talk about it . . . or you can e-mail me back. (Isn't it weird how sometimes it's easier to say things in letters or e-mail?????) And you know that sometimes I talk without thinking first, so this way I can think about what I want to say, write it down, look at it, and then change it if it doesn't come out right. (Life would be so much easier if we could do that with talk too.)

Anyway, here goes:

1. I'm really glad you are here. In some ways letters work, but in others they just don't. Now we know what we look like. (It's not sooooo different, but you've got to admit we're growing up and changing. My bust is getting bigger . . . your hair is getting longer . . . and we act different too. You aren't as scared of everything as you used to be. Remember how when we did crafts at day camp you practiced at home for days before you would make something at camp (so you wouldn't make mistakes in public)? Well, I was so proud of you last night. You

went out on the miniature golf course and just played. (And beat my score!!! Bart's too. . . . And you even joked around. Not as much as you do when it's just us, but some!)

2. I know you are upset about the phone call from your mom. I just wish you weren't having so many problems with your father and that you would let me know what's going on. (You always get so quiet when something is really bothering you!!!) Maybe it's hard to talk with me about your dad because you know how I feel about him, but I wish I could say something that would make you feel better. And here's another thing that's hard to say in person. . . . I get a little jealous when you talk to Barb privately. I think that when I'm with you, the two of you start talking about the baby so I'll leave the room . . . and then when I do, you talk about the other stuff. I'm sorry I get so weirded out by this but I do!

3. Your vacation . . . I am soooo sorry it's almost over. I hate that you're only going to be here a few more days.

4. Our birthdays . . . it's going to be really fun to celebrate them together. August 12th and August 18th. . . . So what if we celebrate a little early? That just means we'll be able to celebrate again on the actual days . . . me here, and you in New Jersey. (Have I mentioned that I wish we still lived in the same town??? Remember how we used to celebrate on August 15th because it was right between our birthdays?) Anyway, I'm not going to whine about it. We'll have a great party . . . you and me and my parents.

I guess that's all for now.

I'm going to join you and Barb in the kitchen. Maybe you'll be talking about something besides the FS . . . Future Sibling.

XXX Tara★Starr

Date: July 18 5:34:28 PM
From: Eliz812
Subj: My father
To: TSTARR

Dear Tara,

I'm going to respond to your e-mail thoughts in order, since I like order and a focus for things.

1. First of all, I'm really glad I'm here too! This is a great vacation. Even with the news about Dad it's a great vacation. I've missed you so much that I almost can't believe I'm here with you. Does it seem like I've been here for five days already? Not to me. It feels like I just got here yesterday. And yes, you and I are changing — in good ways. I'm glad you think I'm a little more outgoing. I think you're a little

calmer. And I think you're starting to accept that you ARE the kid in your family, not the parent. You should enjoy that while you can. Being the parent is a lot of responsibility. I should know. I feel like Emma's parent most days now, even though Mom tries hard not to let me feel that way. (I know that will change in September when Emma and I are back in school.)

2. Yes, the call from Mom did upset me. But the reason I'm not talking about it is because I simply want to enjoy being on vacation while I'm here. I don't want to waste all my time thinking about Dad. I'll be doing enough of that when I get back home. But now that I'm finally with you again, I just want to eat ice cream, and play miniature golf, and goof around with you and your friends, and laugh with you and Barb and Luke. We only have two days left. Why waste them worrying about Dad? You know I'll send you e's about him when I'm home again.

For the record, Mom didn't tell me anything new about Dad. All she said was that he called a few nights ago and he was drunk. I don't know where he was calling from or why he called or anything. Just that he was drunk, which upset Mom and made her cry.

Tara, I wish SO MUCH that Dad hadn't gotten in touch with us again. When he left (and it's SO hard to believe that that was just a couple of months ago) I was upset at first, of course, but now I'm glad he's out of our lives. Everything is so much easier and calmer and more predictable without him. It's more orderly and more focused. (See? I really do like order and focus.) There's no more wondering whether Dad's going to come home, whether he's going to be drunk, whether he's going to spend $$ we don't have. Mom and Emma and I are a good family without him. We pay our bills on time, we eat nice normal meals at nice regular hours. We are stable. Emma and I are starting to feel safe again.

And now he's back. Dad is like the scary guy who turns up in those *Halloween* movies JUST when you thought he was finally gone.

Maybe the phone call is all we'll hear from him. Maybe he only wanted to say hi to us. I hope so. I don't ever want to see him again.

Okay, that's enough about Dad for now. But I do promise, Tara, that I won't shut you out where Dad, or anything else, is concerned.

About talking to Barb — I do NOT talk to her about the baby just to get you out of the room. I talk to her about the baby because I'm so excited. Then you leave the room because we're talking about the baby, and then Barb and I continue to talk about the baby, not about anything else. Okay? (You COULD stay and talk with us, you know.)

3. Vacation — I think I covered this in #1.

4. Our birthdays — I can't wait until tomorrow night! Our party is going to be excellent.

Okay. This is a VERY long e, so I'll stop here.

Talk to you in a minute!

Love,

Elizabeth

Date: July 20 12:07:17 PM
From: TSTARR
Subj: Yag. You're gone!!!!!!!!!!!!!!!!!!!!!!!!!!!!!!!
To: Eliz812

I can't believe it. You are on the plane . . . on your way back home.

I just had to e-mail you the second we got back from the airport.

It's so weird.

I was soooooooooooo used to e-mailing you and then being able to talk with you in person right away.

I know. I know. We stopped doing that after your long e-mail about your dad and the call. We decided just to talk face-to-face as long as we could do that . . . and now we can't.

Let me tell you that I miss you already. So does Luke. On the way back he said he felt like we'd had a visit from the "calm patrol." He knows how much you like being "organized and focused" and how much we all learn from you in that area. Barb mentioned how much we give you. (I think she was feeling guilty about not being so organized and focused.) She said we bring out your sense of play and humor, and we help you become more spontaneous, that this is a great friendship for us . . . for you and for me, and for them too.

All I know is that I miss you, and my room misses you. The trundle bed is back under my bed. My clothes are thrown around the way they usually are. My bed is un-made, the way it usually is. (I made it while you were here because I felt guilty that you would make it if I didn't.) And the two dresser drawers, which your clothes were so neatly placed in, are just waiting for my clothes to be thrown back in.

Barb misses you a lot. She cried in the car after we dropped you off. I know she's worried about you, about how it's going to be for you when you get home. (I hope your father NEVER NEVER NEVER calls your house again!!!!!!!!!!!) And I know the little critter, my Future Sibling, misses you . . . misses the way you patted IT by way of Barb's stomach . . . read IT *Good-night Moon* . . . told IT about *Little House on the Prairie*. (When IT is born, maybe I'll read IT *Where the Wild Things Are*.)

Elizabeth, you did have a good time, didn't you? A really good time? I know there were moments when my messiness got on your nerves (probably the same times your neatness got on my nerves) and times when you just wanted to go to sleep and I wanted to stay up talking for hours. Plus, my friends sometimes stopped over without calling first. (I want you to know that I did ask them to do that less while you were here.) I do know you had a great time being able to watch *Wheel of Fortune* again. (Even if I do call the contestants names when they can't figure the puzzles out quickly.)

I guess in some ways we'll both be glad to have things back to "normal," to be able to spend time with our friends and our families in our own space. But Elizabeth, I really am going to miss you a lot.

We did have fun at our birthday party, didn't we?????!!!!!!

I love, lovE, loVE, lOVE, LOVE the present you made for me. It must have taken you forever to cross-stitch

T★STARR onto that material and to decorate the frame with stars and @s. It's truly the most wonderful e-mail name thing I've ever seen. I'm going to hang it on my bedroom door right above the ENTER AT YOUR OWN RISK sign.

I hope you love my presents too. Someday your picture will really be on the calendar with all of the women writers on it. (I feel a little bad about covering over Charlotte Brontë's picture with yours, but she's dead, so she'll never find out!!!!!!!!) And I hope you really like all that sewing stuff I gave you. (Barb helped me pick it out. There was a pair of earrings that I thought were wonderful but Barb said you would rather have the sewing thingamabobs and I should give you what you would really use . . . that the blinking earrings were not something you would wear. I was sooooo glad she gave them to me for my birthday.)

So now you are gone.

I can't wait for your next e-mail.

Love,
Tara★Starr

Date: July 20 9:45:52 PM
From: Eliz812
Subj: Back Home
To: TSTARR

Dear Tara,

I can't believe I'm home again. Our visit is over, my vacation is over, and I'm home again. How did the time go by so quickly? It passed in a blur.

Yes, our birthday celebration was great. I'm glad you liked the present I made you. I loved the sewing things. And I'm REALLY glad YOU were the one who wound up with those earrings.

Hey, Tara, I thought I was the worrier, but you worry about a lot of things too. Like whether I think you're messy or whether I had fun or whether you kept me up too late. You shouldn't worry so much. Not where

I'm concerned. We are best friends. I know we've had fights and things in the past (who hasn't?), but I think we are friends 4-ever.

Well, okay, now here's the news I know you're waiting for. About my father. Mom and I had a talk about him just a little while ago, as soon as Emma went to bed. Now that I'm home and my vacation is over I feel ready to find out about whatever happened the other day. So I asked Mom to give me all the details about the phone call.

This is what she said. Dad called at about 6:30, when Mom and Emma were eating dinner. I'm sure he called at dinnertime on purpose, because he could be pretty sure we'd be home. Mom said she could tell right away that he was drunk. He was slurring his words and everything. (It was only 6:30, Tara. Do you suppose he's drunk all day now?) Well, anyway, that was the first time he had called since he "disappeared," so of course Mom threw question after question at him. Where was he? Was he okay? Why hadn't he come back? Did he know what he was doing to Emma and me? Did he have any money? Was he planning to come back?

I guess Dad was so drunk that he couldn't really answer the questions, and that was when Mom started to cry. Finally she asked him WHY he was calling. I mean, she just wanted to know if he was nearby and was planning to visit us, if he needed something, if he intended to move back in with us. But he couldn't even answer that question. All he said was, "I love all of you." Then he hung up.

So Mom still doesn't know where he is, what happened, what he's living on. She doesn't know a thing.

I hope he's not planning to come back, Tara. What if he's living really close by? What if he even, like, spies on us sometimes? You know, just to see Emma and me. I don't think he does, but you never know. Mom is freaked out, I can tell. So am I.

You know what? All we know for sure after that phone call is that Dad isn't dead.

And I wish he were.

Love,
Elizabeth

Dear Elizabeth,

I'm sorry I didn't answer your e-mail right away, but it was really late when I got home last night and Barb said (after a very long lecture . . . I'll explain that in a minute) that I had to go to bed. She said I couldn't even check to see if you had written and that I better "get my butt in bed pronto."

You can tell from that quote that Barb and Luke are not pleased with me.

Here's what happened.

Hannah called early yesterday morning and asked me to come over.

So I did.

Hannah's older sister Nan just got her driver's license last week. Their parents had gone away for a few days and left Nan in charge, and Hannah and Nan decided they wanted to go to their lake house for the day. (Isn't it cute that they both have names that are palindromes?)

So I called Barb and Luke to ask permission, but I couldn't reach either one of them at work.

Hannah and Nan said that we should leave right away because it was almost two hours to the lake and we should get there in time for sun and swimming. So I borrowed one of Hannah's bathing suits and we left.

I was going to call Barb and Luke again (well, I tried once but still no answer), and then we were having such a good time that I forgot. I just forgot . . . until around four or five.

When I called, Barb and Luke were angry . . . really angry . . . really really angry . . . and said I had to come back "RIGHT NOW."

So even though it ruined the rest of our day at the lake, we all came back.

Elizabeth, we got caught in a bad traffic jam. (It was nervous-making because Nan was very tense in the jam. I guess that's because she just got her license and isn't used to everything.) And then we got a flat tire, which none of us knew how to fix so we had to wait for help. (That was also nervous-making because while we waited some weird guys stopped and offered to help.) Then a police car stopped and the guys left. (That was a little scary too because the police ran a check on us to make sure everything was legal. . . . Even though Nan looks like she's about twelve years old, she really is seventeen.) Anyway, since their parents were out of town and Nan was supposed to be "watching" Hannah, the police couldn't reach their parents. So it all took a lot of time.

Then the police officers decided to call my parents. Needless to say, Barb and Luke were not happy by the time I got home.

So now I have to stay in the house for the next three days . . . no television . . . and I have even more rules that I have to live by. (I'm sorry I forgot to call them again in the afternoon, but I guess I knew they might not like the idea of my being in a car driven by someone who had just gotten her license.)

Anyway, that's why I didn't answer your e-mail right away.

About your e-mail. . . . Wow. I don't know what to say. It sounds awful. Your dad sounds really scary. Can't your mom make him stop calling? Can't someone make him go to one of those places for alcoholics?

And I've never heard you say something like that about him.

I'm sorry things are so bad. E-mail me soon.

Love,
Tara★Starr

Date: July 22 3:56:37 PM
From: Eliz812
Subject: Tara's Big Adventure
To: TSTARR

Dear Tara★Starr,

It's 4:00 on a really, really, REALLY hot day. I took Emma to the pool this morning and she caught up with a bunch of her little friends — Matt and some other kids — so we spent most of the day there. We only went home long enough for lunch (there is a snack bar at the pool, but it's cheaper to fix sandwiches at home). Anyway, the good thing is that Emma wore herself out at the pool and is now . . . NAPPING. So I took a few minutes to check my e-mail, and there was your letter.

Oh. My. God. Have Barb and Luke ever grounded you before? I can't remember that happening. I have to say, Tara, that even though your adventure sounds like a lot of fun, I'm not sure I'd have gone off with someone who just got her license. I'm not scolding you. All I'm trying to say is . . . do you know how complicated it is to drive a car? The dashboard alone scares me, not to mention all the things under the hood. I'm not sure I WANT to drive when I get old enough. I think I'll leave that to people with lots and lots of experience. Professionals. Such as bus drivers.

Anyway. Are you speaking to Barb and Luke? Are they speaking to you? If you are speaking, is it in that stiff, mad way, or a more normal way? At least they didn't take away computer privileges. We can still send each other e-mail (lots of it) in the next few days.

Oh, just for the record — you asked me if we can't make my father stop calling. I want to point out (just so you won't worry about something unnecessarily) that he has only called that one time while I was visiting you. I said I was <u>afraid</u> he'd keep calling, but he hasn't. And I was simply <u>wondering</u> if he might spy on us. I mean, I just made that up. We haven't heard from him since the phone call. So I am keeping my fingers crossed. I want him to stay away.

What I'm going to say next might seem like a strange thing to say after a year in which so many awful things have happened, but this summer I feel happier than I've felt in a long time. I feel so settled. My life seems so nice and ordinary now. I don't have to worry about bill collectors or moving or Dad sitting around drunk in his underwear ordering stuff we can't afford from the home shopping channel. It's just Mom and Emma and me, all calm and cozy. Mom works, we have enough $$ to afford our apartment, and Emma and I have friends here at DEER RUN. . . .

Speaking of friends, remember when I told you that Howie and Susie and I were going to start our own poetry workshop this summer, and have ice-cream night and all those things? Well, we haven't actually managed a regular ice-cream night (although we do run over to the Dair-E Freez every now and then, where the cheapest cone you can get costs just 65 cents, so I don't feel too extravagant), but we did start the workshop! We met last night for the first time. We decided to start with the poetry of Langston Hughes, since one of his poems inspired the name of our journal. (Can you believe that I can't WAIT for school to start because I can't wait to begin working on the next issue of *Silhouette*?) Anyway, right after I got back from Ohio, Howie and Susie and I went to the library and we each checked out a different book about Langston Hughes. Then we met last night at Howie's house to talk about Hughes and his poems. It was SO COOL and would only have been better if we'd been wearing black berets and drinking coffee, but none of us owns a beret OR likes coffee. We're going to talk about Hughes again at our next meeting, then move on to Robert Frost (SO different).

Well, I can hear Emma rustling around in our room. (Just so you can imagine where things are in the apartment, the computer is in the living room since it's the family computer, like yours is, and Mom needs it too.)

Anyway, I better go check on Emma. She usually wakes up fussy. Write again as soon as you can and tell me what's going on. And if you're bored, write often!

Love,
Elizabeth

Date: July 23 8:42:29 AM
From: TSTARR
Subj: Greetings From the Grounded
To: Eliz812

I hate being grounded. I can't see anyone. It's summer and I have to stay inside . . . no television . . . no being with friends . . . and after today, I am grounded for another full day. And no, Elizabeth, I've never been grounded before.

It's not fair. I made a mistake. I should've called before I left. (But I *really really* wanted to go and I knew Barb and Luke would have said no.) I'm only a kid . . . and no one is perfect. So I think I should have just gotten off with a warning.

The only good thing about this grounding is that I have some reading time . . . and I'm going to read Langston

Hughes' poetry so I can pretend to be part of your workshop. (So I'm a little jealous that you and Howie and Susie are doing that. I can't get anyone here to read poetry. Although going out for ice cream is something the group here WILL do.)

Elizabeth, I can't believe you don't want to get a driver's license the second you are old enough to have one. I CAN'T WAIT until I'm old enough. There are so many places I want to go to. And it'll be great not to have to depend on Barb and Luke.

I hope your father NEVER EVER calls you again . . . that he never bothers you, your mom, or Emma.

Yesterday, Barb went to the doctor and was told that the DS (Demon Seed, Darling Sibling) will be born around Christmas. Barb and Luke keep talking about what a great present the baby will be. I feel like it will be a lump of coal. As much as I try to feel different, I really don't like the idea of having a baby brother or sister. Please tell me why you think it's such a great idea. I know how much you love Emma (and don't get me wrong — I think she's a great kid . . . to visit), but WHY, OH WHY, OH WHY should I, a thirteen-year-old, want to have a baby brother or sister? (I keep thinking that Barb was only four years older than I am when she got pregnant with me.) I am so afraid the baby will make me feel like I'm grounded . . . that I'll have to stay in and take care of it a lot . . . that I'll have to be a good example for it. . . .

I'm going to save up my money so that I can come visit you when the baby is born. It'll be Christmas vacation, so if you have the room, I'll have the time. What do you think??????????????????????????????????????

Groundedly yours,
Tara★Starr

Date: July 28 7:38:56 PM
From: Eliz812
Subj: Dad
To: TSTARR

Dear Tara★Starr,

It's Wednesday night and I wanted a little time alone, time to myself, so Mom has taken Emma to Chuck E. Cheese for pizza and playtime. This was great of Mom, since she comes home from work so tired. But tomorrow is my night with Emma, and Mom can have time to herself.

I'm sorry it's taken me so long to write to you again. Your groundation is over by now (unless it got extended for some reason). I had visions of us furiously writing back and forth, back and forth, to help you pass the time. What happened was that not long after I wrote to you about the poetry workshop and all . . . Dad called again. And he said he wanted to come visit Mom and Emma and me. I don't know why we believed him. I mean, the last time he said he was going to come by, he arranged to come when we wouldn't be here. But this sounded different. The last time, he hadn't said he wanted to <u>visit</u> us; he had just said he was going to pick up his things. But when he called over the weekend he specifically said he wanted to SEE us. And he was crying. He said he missed us and couldn't believe how long it had been and even apologized for coming by when we weren't home before.

So this time we expected him to show up. Mom invited him for dinner on Monday night. (I heard her whisper to him that he better show up sober.) Then she made the mistake of telling Emma what was going to happen. I mean, it all sounded so . . . real that Mom decided to prepare Emma for the visit.

Emma, of course, was beside herself with excitement and wanted to help Mom plan the dinner menu. (Her suggestion: pasketti, ice cream, and Hawaiian Punch. Final menu: salmon steaks, asparagus, salad, and ice cream.) Dad was supposed to arrive at 6:00 on Monday night. At 6:30 he hadn't shown up and Emma abandoned her post at the window and watched a video instead. At 7:00 he hadn't shown up and Emma was starving so she ate her dinner. At 8:00 he hadn't shown up and Mom and I were starving so we ate our dinners, and Emma was crabby so Mom got her ready for bed. Finally, a little before 9:00, two things happened at once. Mom put Emma to bed, screaming and kicking (literally) because she was disappointed and overtired, and the phone rang and I answered it. It was Dad.

Tara, I was SO angry at him. All I said was, "Where ARE you? You ruined Emma's night."

Well, he was so drunk I couldn't understand his answer. I was just about to slam the phone down without saying good-bye when Mom rushed into the kitchen and took the phone from me and started YELLING at Dad. When she finally stopped there was this long pause, then she said very quietly. "Okay, fine," and hung up.

Neither Mom nor I know exactly what happened, why he didn't show up. Our guess is that he was afraid to, for some reason. Like, maybe he can't face us. He's still ashamed of all that happened. But nights like this aren't going to help things.

Anyway, this is why Mom and I are still sort of recovering and why we want time to ourselves. I told Howie and Susie what happened, of course, and we went out for ice cream last night, but tonight I just wanted to be alone. And to write and tell you what's going on.

Are you enjoying the Langston Hughes poetry? We're LOVING it and are thinking about staying with it for one more week before moving on to Robert Frost. Do you have a favorite Hughes poem yet?

About the baby — of course you can come visit us at Christmas (well, I suppose I should check with Mom, but I don't see why you couldn't come), but Tara, I really think you'll want to get to know your little sister or brother after the baby comes home from the hospital. What do I like about having a little sister? Almost everything. Emma has her bad times, but her tantrums and messes and endless questions are more than made up for by the wonderfulness of herself. Do you know what it's like to live with a little person who ADORES you? Who looks up to you and wants to be with you and be like you? I love reading to her and teaching her things and taking her places. And dressing her. Tara, you'll like dressing the baby. You love to dress people. Think of the baby as a sartorial playground.

All right, Mom and Emma will be back soon and I want to take a bath and read in the tub while I still have the chance, so I'll sign off now.

Love,
Elizabeth

Date: August 3 10:22:41 AM
From: TSTARR
Subj: News — Yours and Mine
To: Eliz812

Dear Elizabeth,
Grounding is over. It lasted for the three days . . . and then Barb and Luke said I had learned my lesson. (I have. I really have. So has Nan. So has Hannah.) Hannah's parents and mine had a meeting with Hannah and Nan and me, and then, believe it or not, they all decided I could still go to the lake with their family for a week . . . so I went. But there's no computer there, so I couldn't get or send e-mail. I did send a postcard. (Remember the "old days" before e-mail????????)

Anyway, I did not get back until late last night (very sunburned) and didn't read my e-mail until this morning (very tired).

Elizabeth, your news is sad . . . and very very angry-making!!!!!!!!!!!!!!!!!!!!!!! I wish someone would just take your father and put him in some place where he could "dry out," get sober, grow up. Maybe he should go to the place that president's wife set up, the Betty Ford Clinic. (I saw something about it on TV.) A lot of famous people go there. And then he would leave you and your mom alone. I hope you don't mind my mentioning this, but that same TV show mentioned AA, Alcoholics Anonymous, and the AA groups that help the family members of alcoholics. One group is called Alateen. Maybe you should see if there's one near you. That may help. And there's one for your mom. Don't get mad that I mentioned this. I know that sometimes you think I get too dramatic about stuff, but I don't think I'm doing that this time. I'm really worried about you. I do think it's good that you are SO angry.

I'm glad you have Howie and Susie to talk with. To be honest, it was kind of hard to read that you told them what was going on first . . . but I'll get over it.

I'm not sure which Langston Hughes poem I like best. Maybe the one about the caged bird. What do you think of that one???

About visiting at Christmas . . . thanks for letting me know it's a possibility. Sometimes I feel really closed in here, thinking about the baby. Am I going to have to take care of it a lot? (I know that Barb said no . . . but she works and goes to school. Duh.) I've thought about what you said. It would be nice to have a little nerdlet in the house who absolutely adores me . . . which, if it is a girl, I can teach to accessorize. And now that I'm getting older (and so are my parents), I feel like Barb and Luke are getting stricter. Maybe with the baby they won't have as much time to worry about me. (That's sort of a plus and a minus at the same time.)

I'm going to go peel some of my sunburned skin off right now. I know that sounds gross . . . but you should see me. I look like my body is unraveling. I love peeling skin off. I try to take it off in long strips. It's soooooooooooooo disgusting. Is it weird that I like doing that????????

With my sunburn . . . and all the books I read while I was at the lake . . . I am not only well-read, I'm well-red.

Love,
Tara★

67

Date: August 5 11:35:51 AM
From: Eliz812
Subj: A Rainy Day
To: TSTARR

Dear Tara★Starr,

It's a rainy day . . . totally pouring. And it's so dark and foggy you can hardly see. Luckily, Matt wanted to play with Emma, so Susie walked him over here this morning. The three of us are in the living room now. Matt and Emma are playing their own version of Candy Land, which doesn't even involve the board from the game. They're just pretending they live in a land filled with candy and can eat whatever they want whenever they want. What a shock they're going to have at lunchtime when I serve them chicken noodle soup and apples.

Anyway, I can keep writing to you as long as the kids keep entertaining themselves.

Yes, I'm REALLY mad at Dad. We haven't heard from him since the night he didn't show up. I suppose we should consider ourselves lucky that he called to say he wasn't going to arrive. At least he did that. You know something? We still don't know where Dad is living or what he's doing, what he's living on, but since he at least calls from time to time we don't worry about him so much anymore. It's not like when he first left and no one had heard from him. I imagine he lives somewhere nearby, but I have no idea where. And what do you suppose he's living on? I mean, where is he getting $$? He certainly doesn't ask us for any, not that we have any extra to give him.

Tara, you should really be more careful with the sun. Did you know that just a few bad sunburns can lead to SKIN CANCER? I'm not kidding. Mom and Emma and I never get sunburns anymore. I slather Emma and myself with waterproof sunblock every day of the summer, whether we're going to the pool or not. (Well, I don't put it on us on a day like today.) And at the pool we always wear hats and big, long T-shirts except for when we go in the water. We may appear a little pasty by the end of the summer, but I don't care. I can't help but look at really tan people and think, "Someday they're probably going to get skin cancer." I don't want to scare you, but be more careful — at least for my sake. I want us to be friends forever and ever, even when we're ninety and doddering in rocking chairs on a front porch somewhere.

Yes, I have heard of Alateen, and also Al-Anon. I even looked them up in the phone book after I got your e-mail AND I made a couple of phone calls. I found out that there are Alateen meetings over in Stockton. That's not TOO far away. It's something to think about.

I LOVE that you're reading Langston Hughes too! That is so cool. You can be the Ohio branch of our workshop. My favorite Hughes poem is still "Mother to Son." Sometimes I look at it and just read and reread those first few lines over and over. They give me a lump in my throat.

Yesterday I was in an autumn frame of mind (probably because of all the back-to-school stuff in the stores) and I wrote this poem about trees in late fall:

Pride

Tall white birches
Stretch stately fingers
Up to the sky.

The wind ruffles
Their few dry, brown leaves
But not their pride.

Uh-oh. Candy Land has erupted into a shouting match. Maybe it's time for lunch.

More later.

Love,
Elizabeth

P.S. Howie and Susie and I are talking about having a little party. We're just thinking of inviting ourselves — but we see each other all the time. Is this a weird idea?

Date: August 6 10:52:03 AM
From: TSTARR
Subj: Shopping for the DS
TO: Eliz812

Dear Elizabeth,

Sorry this is going to be a short e but Barb and Luke and I are going out in a few minutes . . . checking out the garage sales. We are shopping for the Baby formerly known as "It." Since the Baby is not due until December, we really don't have to shop now, in the summer, in August . . . but in the winter there won't be as many chances to shop secondhand. (No garage sales or lawn sales with snow on the ground.) Anyway, it means that if we find stuff, we'll just trip over it from now until December. You know how little storage space there is in this apartment. It'll be a constant reminder to me that life is going to change.

It really dawned on me this morning that I'm going to have to share my room with this creature . . . this baby . . . this crying pooping thing. Barb and Luke say the baby will be in their bedroom for a long time . . . but knowing them, they are going to want their privacy. Yikes!!!!!!!!!!!!!!!!!!!!

To quickly mention the things in your e:

I promise to be more careful in the sun. It was an accident. I fell asleep. I will never do that again. (I will fall asleep, just not in the sun at noon.)

I'm glad you checked out **Alateen**, etc. Let me know what happens with that (if you want to tell me).

I think it's great that the three of you are going to have a party. It's never silly to celebrate friends!!!!!!!

Gotta go. . . . Luke is honking the horn.

Bye for now.
Tara★Starr

Date: August 12 9:38:48 PM
From: Eliz812
Subj: My Birthday (And More)
To: TSTARR

Dear Tara,

How did a whole week go by since I received your e-mail? So much is happening here — some of it good, some of it bad. I'm trying to figure out how to organize my thoughts. I think I'll tell you the things in the order in which they happened. But before I begin, how did shopping for the Baby go? Hey, have you and Barb and Luke been thinking about baby names yet? I know I asked about this before, but now there are only four months to go, and I'm dying to know the possibilities. How about Elizabeth for a girl? (Just kidding.)

Okay, here's what's been going on, and also why it's taken me so long to get back to you:

Howie and Susie kept asking me about having a little party, the one I mentioned to you in my last e. I thought a party was a nice idea and all (and I LOVED what you said about celebrating friends), but I couldn't figure out why they were so insistent that we choose the evening on which to hold it. They wouldn't stop asking me about it, though, so finally I suggested we hold it on Tuesday (two nights ago), in place of our poetry workshop. They kind of glanced at each other and then Susie said, "What's wrong with Wednesday night?" and Howie said, "Or better yet, Thurs —" but Susie elbowed him, and he didn't finish his sentence. In the end we decided to have it on Wednesday. Considering that it was supposed to be this casual get-together, they were awfully nervous about it. They kept saying to me, "You're sure you're free on Wednesday?" and "Wednesday isn't going to change at the last minute, is it?" Things like that. Tara, I swear, I just wasn't thinking. Otherwise I might have figured it out. But I couldn't think about it too much because on Tuesday, Dad intervened again.

You're not going to believe this. That afternoon, just before Mom was due home from work, our doorbell rang, and when I peeked through the peephole . . . there was Dad. For a few seconds I just stood there with my mouth hanging open. I couldn't figure out what to do. I wasn't sure I was supposed to let him in. On the other hand, he's my <u>father</u>. He's one of my <u>parents</u>. Why shouldn't I let him in? Up until a few months ago we lived with him. And Mom had invited him over for dinner and everything. I stood there thinking for so long that he rang the bell again. And I opened the door.

Right away I wished I hadn't, because I could tell he was drunk. He was sort of swaying. And his eyes were red and watery. When he saw me he held his hand out to me. I didn't reach for it. I just stared at him. And then Emma appeared behind me. She looked from Dad to me and back to Dad, but she didn't say anything. Tara, I had absolutely no idea what to say, so I was totally relieved when Mom drove her car into our parking space just then. Mom got out of the car, saw what was going on, and the only (the ONLY) words she said were, "Don't <u>ever</u> come here drunk again. I mean it."

So Dad turned around and walked away. And that was his whole visit. He didn't say a word.

I was freaked out. It's no wonder I didn't realize what Howie and Susie had planned for Wednesday. Not until I rang Susie's bell the next night (we'd decided to have the party at her apartment) and she threw open the door and she and Howie cried, "Happy birthday!" Tara, they'd planned a <u>birthday</u> party for me. They'd decorated Susie's living room with streamers and balloons, and gotten a cake and presents and everything. Most of the presents were silly, jokey things, but they had also pooled their money to get me this BEAUTIFUL hardcover book of Langston Hughes poems. I was SO happy. I practically floated back to our apartment later.

Today is my actual birthday, of course, and I've been thinking about our early celebration last month. Mom and Emma and I went out to dinner tonight, and when we came back we had presents and cake. I just finished opening my gifts. Now Mom is putting Emma to bed. As soon as I finish this letter I am going to begin a new embroidery project. Mom gave me this big book of embroidery stitches (some that you can do with silk ribbon; I'll show you sometime) and lots of materials for embroidery and cross-stitching. (I know, I know, your eyes are glazing over.)

Anyway, it turned out to be a great birthday.

And that's the news of the week.

Lots of Love,
Elizabeth

Date: August 13 11:50:31 AM
From: TSTARR
Subj: Celebrations and Not-so-Celebrations
TO: Eliz812

Dear Elizabeth,
This has to be a fast e because I have to go baby-sit. Yes, that's right . . . baby-sit. Hard to believe, huh????!!!! One of Barb's friends from work is having a problem. Her regular baby-sitter has a cold or the plague or something, so I'm going to help out for a few days. (One four-month-old baby and a three-year-old. I hope I live through it!!!!!!!!) Oh, well, it will be good money, which I can definitely use with school starting soon and clothes to buy. And it will be good practice for being with an actual B . . . as in Baby. Yikes!!!!!!!! Wish me luck!!!!!!! Wish those kids luck!!!!!!!

Your birthday celebration sounds wonderful. Howie and Susie are such good friends for you. (Any romance happening between you and Howie????????????????? Just wondering.)

As for your father . . . Yow. . . . Ouch. . . . I'm so glad your mom showed up when she did . . . scary and awful. Poor you. Poor Emma. How did he get to your house????? He didn't drive there, did he????????? I hope not!!!!!!!!!!!!

Gotta go. I'll send you a report of how my baby-sitting adventure went. Baby-sitting . . . you know that's not something I ever wanted to do. I know you like it, but I wish I could work in a clothing or jewelry store. As soon as I'm old enough that's what I want to do.

Really gotta go. Luke's dropping me off at the lady's house. (He's on his way to class!!!!!!)

Lots of Love . . . and happy day after your birthday, Tara ★

Date: August 16 3:47:53 PM
From: Eliz812
Subj: Weekend
To: TSTARR

Dear Tara★,

Well, it was quite a weekend. And now it's over and we're back to normal (well, normal for summer vacation). Mom is at work and Emma is napping, so I have a few free moments.

All I have to say about this weekend is . . . you just never know. I didn't have any plans for the weekend, so I thought it would just be two days of hanging out. And it was, but not the kind of hanging out I had expected.

On Saturday morning, I was trying to decide whether to lie around on our patio and read, or to call Susie and ask her if she wanted to meet me at the pool . . . when the phone rang. It was Susie wondering if I wanted to take the town bus to the mall and shop for back-to-school stuff. (The great thing about Susie is that she's as broke as I am, so I didn't have to make a big deal out of the fact that I have VERY limited funds.) I said yes, and then Susie asked if Howie could come with us. A boy who wants to go back-to-school shopping? I was skeptical, thinking this might be very much like shopping with Emma, which usually lasts about six minutes. But I said yes, because Howie is nothing if not unusual.

Once we got to the mall, Howie decided he had enough $$ for all his actual supplies — notebooks and pens and stuff. Susie and I decided we had enough $$ for a few supplies and one article of clothing each. I was about to suggest that we split up, and Susie and I go to Old Navy and Howie go to Staples, when Susie suddenly said she just remembered she had to buy a present for someone (she was very vague) and ran off, calling over her shoulder that she'd meet us at Old Navy in half an hour.

So Howie and I went off on our own. About fifteen minutes later, at the exact same moment, we realized what Susie had done. She had purposely left Howie and me alone together. "She's probably spying on us from somewhere," said Howie, glancing around. She wasn't, of course (at least, not that we could see), but we were sure she had tried to set us up.

"Well?" said Howie.

"Well?" I said.

"Well, let's just continue shopping," said Howie.

So we did. And we had a great time. Even though nothing at all happened, except that we stocked up on paper and stuff.

But then yesterday, Howie called and asked me if I wanted to meet him at the pool, which I did. At first I felt bad, like we were leaving Susie out, but then Howie said she and her mom had gone to visit Susie's aunt. Then I felt bad thinking that this was only a Howie-and-me activity by default — even though I don't know WHAT my feelings for Howie are, just that I like the idea of his liking me and wanting to spend time with me alone. Well, not ALONE alone, but you know what I mean.

Or do you, Tara? I'm not sure I know what I mean. This is very confusing.

Anyway, after a couple of hours, Howie and I left the pool and went back to his apartment. His father was out, so we were alone. And even though once again absolutely nothing happened between us, I thought I could feel this very subtle change. Like a change in the atmosphere or something. It was a pleasant change.

And now it is Monday morning and something nice has happened between Howie and me, but I don't even know what it is.

One good thing: Susie and Howie and I are all such great friends that I know I can talk to Susie about this too.

I feel like I'm just blabbering now, so I'll sign off.

Let me know how your baby-sitting job went.

Love,
Elizabeth

Date: August 17 7:45:41 PM
From: Blane
Subj: Where in the World is Tara Starr Lane?
To: Eliz812

Hey, Elizabeth . . . Surprise! It's Barb Lane.

Tara Starr wants me to let you know that she will be unable to send or receive e-mail for several days.

Why? you may ask. . . . Let me tell you!

TARA STARR LANE IS BABY-SITTING. . . . That's right, baby-sitting. Baby-sitting for a three-year-old boy named Dougie and an eight-month-old girl named Sara.

Why is she doing this???? We know it's not because of her great love of babies.

There are several reasons:

1. It's an emergency and she's being a terrific kid and helping out. My friend Natalie is allergic to bee stings and got stung yesterday. She's home from the hospital, but she needs help. So Tara Starr is going to stay with her for a few days. (Natalie's husband is on an overseas business trip and her relatives live in California.)

2. Even though Tara Starr said she would work for nothing, Natalie will be paying her and Tara can use the money to buy the things she considers essential that her parents don't . . . like glitter notebooks and fluffy purple pens.

3. I think Tara Starr is glad to have a vacation from her parents!!!

So there you have it . . . why it will be next to impossible to contact Tara Starr for two days. (Did I mention that Natalie doesn't have a computer????)

Anyway, Luke and I are sending you lots of hugs and hope you and your mom and sister are doing well.

Tara Starr will be in touch as soon as possible.

As always,
Barb

Date: August 21 3:16:53 PM
From: TSTARR
Subj: I'm baaaaaaaaaaaaaaaaack
To: Eliz812

Dear Elizabeth,

I'm home.
I'm sooooooooooooooooooooo tired.

I wish that little kids came equipped with batteries that could be taken out when they need to calm down. Dougie, the three-year-old, never stopped!!!!!!!! I made up ribbons to give to him as prizes when he did something right . . . first-place ones for going to bed on time, making it to the potty on time, not bothering Tara★. . . . He didn't get too many of those. I should have made ones that said: #1 at Temper Tantrums, #1 at Stalling at Bedtime, #1 at Driving Tara★ Nuts. If I'd made those up, he would have gotten a lot more ribbons. Actually, there were moments he was human and even kind of lovable. And he was soooooooooooo good when I read to him. I just loved rereading all my old favorite books. What great characters. Remember George and Martha, and Max from *Where the Wild Things Are,* and Arthur? And I just LOVE Frog and Toad.

As for the baby, she sure is a puker and she can cry very loudly when she's angry. Since her mom was sick, she couldn't be fed the way she is used to being fed. (Nothing I could do to help with that one!!!!!) But I did give her bottles and she was kind of cute when she drank and held on to one of my fingers. The best thing about her is that she doesn't tell stupid knock-knock jokes. (If Dougie told me the Boo Who one once more, I was going to have to scream.) You know what else is fun??? As long as you use a nice voice, you can say almost anything to a baby and watch her grin. I would say things like "You are a total nerdlet." And "When you grow up, you're going to get a tattoo." And she laughed!

So I survived it. Don't think I don't know that even though Natalie DID need help, it was part of a plot to get me used to babies. And who knows . . . even though I don't get warm and goo-goo when I see one, I managed to survive the experience. (All right, I admit it . . . it actually was OK sometimes!!! But that's all I will admit.)

Oh, well . . . enough about that.

Now on to the important things.

While I was baby-sitting, a monumental thing happened. I BECAME A TEENAGER. OK . . . I know that you became one six days before me, so you are probably used to being one, but it's new to me. Anyway, don't get too proud of becoming a teenager first. You'll also become a senior citizen first. (Actually I've never seen you toooooo proud, but anyway . . .) On my birthday, Barb and Luke came over to Natalie's house with an ice-cream cake and we celebrated that way . . . but I'm going to be able to celebrate again. . . . There's going to be another party when Hannah gets back from the lake and when BART gets back from exercising his cute body at tennis camp. We're going to get together with the "gang" and have a combination Tara★ Birthday and Back-to-School Bash. Three celebrations for one birthday is a pretty good deal, huh? Wish you could be here.

I am so glad Bart is coming back. I've missed him sooooooooo much. The only kissing I've been doing lately is with Dougie . . . and when I kiss him on the forehead, he screams, "Girl germs!" and then wipes the kiss off. But he keeps coming back for more.

Speaking of kissing . . . hmmmmmm. Just what is happening between you and Howie???????? Last e-mail you said things were changing!!!!! So tell me all. . . . Ask me all. (If there is something major that you have questions about, you can always ask Barb. She'll be glad to explain. It's a little embarrassing at first, but then it's pretty interesting!!!!!!!!)

Love,
Tara★

Date: August 26 4:02:54 PM
From: Eliz812
Subj: Naptime
To: TSTARR

Dear Tara★Starr,

Ahhh, naptime. Emma's, that is. The longer the summer goes on, the more I look forward to her naptime. I still love taking care of Emma, but I've been at the job for two months now, and, well, naptime has taken on a special meaning for me. Unless Mom takes Emma out in the evening, it's usually the only time I really have to myself each day. (You know how much I like living at DEER RUN, how much better things are than they were when Dad was around, but I do miss having my own room.)

Anyway . . . so you baby-sat. HA! I can't believe it. I'm glad it went well. Now when we write we can exchange sitting tips, arts-and-crafts ideas, child-friendly recipes. Do you know what "ants on a log" is? (Yes, it's a recipe.) Tara, if you survived three days in charge of TWO kids, one of them a baby, then you can certainly survive the arrival of one sibling. Wouldn't your job have been easy (well, a lot easier) if you'd only had to care for Sara? And when the B_____ arrives, you won't have full-time charge of it anyway. You can probably work things out so you only get to do the fun things, like dress the B_____, play with her, tell her she's a nerdlet — then turn her over to Barb and Luke when she's crying or needs her diaper changed. (Can you tell that I hope the B_____ is a girl?)

I don't KNOW what is happening between Howie and me. That's why I asked you to help me out. I know that wasn't a very specific question (actually, it wasn't even a question), but what do you think? As I said, I like the idea of Howie's liking me and wanting to spend time alone with me, but . . . I don't really know where this is going. Have your feelings for a boy ever changed? Like, first you were just friends with him and gradually you felt a little different? That's what I meant when I asked for your advice.

Anyway, I'm soooooo busy these days — baby-sitting, writing poetry, trying to see Susie and HOWIE in the evenings — so I better go.

More soon.

Love,
Elizabeth

Date: August 31 10:02:15 AM
From: TSTARR
Subj: Guys . . . and the B-word (two separate subjects!!!!!)
To: Eliz812

Dear Elizabeth,
About Howie . . . I guess I need to ask some questions. I hope you don't mind . . . and don't think you need to answer anything you don't want to. I know how shy you are about stuff like this. Anyway . . .

1. What exactly have the two of you done . . . have you really done? So far it's all in your mind. And in your heart. Right?

2. How do you feel "a little different"? Does the new feeling make you nervous? Does it make you happy?

3. Has Howie ever said anything . . . or done anything? As I remember, he is kind of shy too.

To answer your question . . . yes, there are times when my feelings for a boy have changed, but you know me. My feelings change a lot. Usually I fall madly in love with a guy before I know him. Sometimes I end up never talking to him again. Sometimes he never even knows that I am in love with him . . . and my feelings change before he finds out. (That usually happens while I am watching him from across a room and see him pick his nose or scratch his butt or something.) Anyway, I think this is one way we are very different. I can't see you acting the way I do with boys. (That doesn't make one of us right and the other wrong . . . it's just different!!!!!) You are much more cautious. I fall in and out of love a lot. But I really don't think it's real LOVE. After all, I'm only just thirteen, and there's a lot more to real love. I think I just like the drama of it. Well, actually, there are some other things I like about it. But it's a little embarrassing to write about, especially since I know how shy you are. Don't get the wrong idea, though. What I'm talking about are just crushes . . . and some kissy-face. And with Bart, it's more. It started out as this huge romantic crush, and the more I get to know him, the more I like him. He's becoming a real friend as well as "The Boyfriend."

Does any of this help you at all??????????

Now, since you keep mentioning the B-word . . . Barb had a test and the baby is fine. The doctor asked if she wanted to know if it's a boy or a girl, but my parents have decided they want to be surprised . . . they don't care "as long as the baby is healthy." Well, I want to know!!!! Since the little critter is going to be here, I think we should start planning its wardrobe right now. If it's a girl, I have plans for outfits . . . sparkle booties, sequined rubber pants, and a bib with a necklace sewn on to it. This kid is going to have to have fashion flair. I guess I think the baby is a girl too. Let's hope we're right. (Do any of your arts-and-crafts projects show how to make the things I want to make? And while I'm mentioning that . . . what is "ants on a log"????)

Just remember, Elizabeth, even though I am now admitting there is going to be a BABY, that doesn't mean I'm going to turn into THE MOST WONDERFUL SISTER IN THE WORLD. Speaking of which, I have a special project. I've made a graph. On it are the measurements of MY room, my height and weight, and the projected height and weight of the baby. I've also made up a floor plan for who gets what part of the room. Needless to say, the baby gets only a small portion. She can sleep in a little storage crate. (Which I will "craftily" decorate.) After all, I was here first!!!! Tee-hee.

So that's it for now.

Happy almost-time-to-start-a-new-school-year.

Love,
Tara★

Date: August 31 4:17:37 PM
From: Eliz812
Subj: Your News
To: TSTARR

Dear Tara,

I just got your e, and I only have time for a quick re-
ply. I promise a longer e-letter later.

For now:

About Howie — he and I haven't done a thing. It's
just that I think we're beginning to have more emotional feelings about each other. We've always had
fun when we hung out, and I feel like I could talk to
Howie about anything, just like I could talk to you or
Susie about anything. But now . . . I don't know.
There's this funny edge to us, especially when we're
alone together. Like we know something that other

people don't know. But we've never kissed. We've never even held hands.

About the B____ — I like your graph project, but let me just remind you of one thing: Babies come with a lot of equipment. On your graph, make sure to allow space for the crib, a changing table, a dresser, and a rocker (at the very least). These would be the bare essentials for a new baby.

About arts and crafts — I can find you directions and patterns for making all sorts of things. You know what? If you go back to that great fabric store you took me to and look at the back of all the big pattern books, almost every one of them includes a section on crafts. You'll be surprised what fun stuff you can find in there for babies.

Ants on a log — simple and yummy! Just spread peanut butter in a stalk of celery (that's the log) and put raisins on top.

Gotta go. More soon. This is Labor Day weekend, though, and we have a lot of plans, so the next time I write will probably be after SCHOOL has started.

Love,
Elizabeth

Date: September 7 4:57:56 PM
From: Eliz812
Subj: Back to School
To: TSTARR

Dear Tara★,

I can't believe it. School has started again. Eighth grade!!!!! Next year we'll be going to HIGH SCHOOL. That is soooo hard to believe.

Here's a quick rundown of the day. I wore brand-new jeans, a new crop-top cotton sweater (a present from Mom because she said I had done a wonderful job with Emma and with generally helping out all summer), new black shoes (bought with my hard-earned $$), and new earrings. One earring is a piece of cherry pie; from the other dangles a knife, a fork, and a spoon. Howie and Susie and I walked to school together. During my study hall I met with Mrs.

Jackson about *Silhouette* and we are going to hold our first meeting on Friday after school — my staff and I, that is. The staff is pretty much in place from last year, except that we have to give the sixth-graders and any new students the chance to join if they want to. Mrs. Jackson hopes that will happen in the next two weeks. And we are going to push to get our first issue out by the end of October. Isn't that exciting?

I actually have homework tonight. Not too much. The good thing, though, is that Emma started school today too, which means she's back in day care in the afternoons, and she and Mom don't come home until around six, so I have time to myself after school. I have to fix dinner, though. Tara, can you believe that Emma started KINDERGARTEN today? She's at our old elementary school. And get this — she has my old kindergarten teacher. I can't wait to hear her tales of the day.

Okay. I better go start dinner.

Love,
Elizabeth

P.S. Write and tell me about your first day of school. I guess you start tomorrow.

Date: September 9 11:00:54 PM
From: TSTARR
Subj: Back-to-school and other parts of life
To: Eliz812

Yikers! Zounds! Where has the time gone?

Sorry I haven't been in touch for a while but sooooooooooooo much has happened.

The Tara★ Birthday and Back-to-School Bash was super . . . sooooooooooooo much fun. . . . Bart is back. . . . Hannah is back. . . . So are the rest of the kids. . . . I baby-sat a little more. . . . The nerdlets are fine. . . .

Getting ready for school took more time than usual. Even though I didn't buy much, a lot of time was spent at the mall making decisions about a back-to-school wardrobe. (With my limited budget, I didn't get a lot. I just looked a lot.)

I decided to try out a new first-day look. So I wore a skirt. That's right, a SKIRT . . . long black. And I got a longish silky-looking purple shirt to go with it. I wore purple sneakers, lots of jewelry, and a lacy beret kind of thing on my head. If I do say so myself, I looked *trés* sophisticated for my first day of eighth grade. I organized my friends (my girl friends) to dress up for the first day too. It was so much fun.

I've decided to join the yearbook staff this year. Plus, I'll still write my column for the paper. And I'm going to try out for the school play again, only THIS year it's a musical, *Annie*. (I know, I know. I can't carry a tune, but I'll just sing softly if I get a part. In real life, I would die if I were an orphan, but in make-believe it will be fun. Hmmmmm, I wonder if there was ever a star of a musical who didn't sing on key.)

As for homework . . . you are not going to believe our assignment for social studies class. It's for the unit on family. We have to pretend to be grown-ups. And we have to work out budgets, etc., AND we have to take care of babies. (Not real ones, but egg babies.) It's a plot. I bet that somehow Barb and Luke have convinced the school to make me care for a baby. . . . Well, not really, since last year's class had to do the same project. Our teacher, Mr. Izzard, has already as-signed us to families. Hannah is a single mother. Bart is married to this girl Lisa, and they have a bouncing baby egg that they have named Bart Jr. . . . I AM NOT HAPPY ABOUT THIS SITUATION!!!! And obviously the baby egg is not bouncing, although I would like to bounce it. (Okay, I really don't want to hurt an inno-cent baby egg, but Bart should be married to me.) I am married to this new kid, Phil. We have twin eggs. I have not yet given them names. Phil took them home tonight. I told him we would have to share custody, since Mr. Izzard said we are "separated but trying to work things out." This is such a stupid assignment. I don't want to have to take care of an egg as if it were a real child. Tomorrow Mr. Izzard (the gizzard) is going to tell us what our jobs are, etc., and we are going to have to work out a budget. I hope Phil and I make enough money to hire a full-time nanny or to send our children to boarding school.

Hmmm . . . as you know, the B___ in my family (not the make-believe egg one) is due mid-December. Maybe I can convince Barb and Luke to send it to boarding school. Do you think there is a boarding school for newborns? Just a thought. (Oh . . . and I know that the baby is going to take up a lot of space in MY room, but if life was fair it would only get a few square feet to live in.)

Oh, well. . . . Got to sign off to get my outfit ready for tomorrow.

I'm going to wear a long brown skirt, a short beige top, lots of jewelry, and a rhinestone barrette.

Love,
TSTARR

P.S. And my purple sneakers.

Date: September 11 3:42:08 PM
From: Eliz812
Subj: Dad
To: TSTARR

Dear Tara★,

I have done something I have never done before. Not in my whole life. I have lied to my mother. Well, actually, I haven't lied to her, but I haven't told her about something really, really big and important that she would want to know about. I guess that's like a sin of omission instead of a sin of commission. (Is there such a thing as a lie of omission?) Anyway, it's Saturday afternoon and Mom has taken Emma shoe shopping. And here I can tell you about one little piece of good news before I tell you about my lie/sin. Mom got a raise! She wasn't supposed to get a raise until November, but she's doing such a fantastic job with fund-raising for Kate's Kitchen that Kate gave

Mom her raise early. This means two things: 1. Mom no longer needs help from Nana and Grandpa to make ends meet each month. And 2. Mom will have a TEENSY bit of $$ left over at the end of each month for extras. So Emma is at Hulit's right now getting new sneakers and new rain boots.

All right. Now I better tell you what I didn't do. I didn't tell Mom that Dad called yesterday afternoon just after I had gotten home from school. I'm not positive why I haven't told her. Maybe because I know she'd be upset by what he asked for. Maybe because I want to do something mean to my father, even if it will fly back in my face and get me in trouble later (I'll explain that in a minute). Or maybe because I simply don't care about my father anymore and I don't exactly feel like helping him out, especially when it would be a burden for Mom. What happened was that the phone rang yesterday just as I was sitting down to write a poem for *Silhouette.* When I heard the slurred voice on the other end of the line I knew it was Dad. (He called me Elezzabish.) He asked for Mom. I wasn't sure whether Dad knew Mom works at Kate's Kitchen, but just in case he didn't, I wasn't going to be the one to tell him.

THEN he said something like, "How ish she fixed for money?" I didn't know what he was leading up to, so I wasn't sure how to answer that. So then Dad started to tell me he needed a loan, and I said, "Well, too bad. She's not here," and I hung up.

That was yesterday. YESTERDAY, Tara. It's a whole day later, and I haven't told Mom about the phone call. Dad is bound to call again and tell her he spoke to me. Do you think I'll get in trouble? Maybe Mom won't believe him. He's always drunk when he calls.

Well, anyway, get this. I LIKED HURTING MY DAD.

I have so much to tell you, Tara, but this is already a very long e. I'll just make a few quick comments:

— Emma LOVES kindergarten and her teacher. AND . . . she's learning to read. This is going to be so exciting to watch.

— School is great. So far we have added one new staff member to *Silhouette.* She's a sixth-grader.

— Our staff meeting yesterday went fine.

— I like the sound of your new look.

— I can't believe your egg project. I've read about that kind of assignment in books, but I've never known anyone who actually had to do it. How are things going with Phil? How are things with you and Bart? Have you named the eggs yet? (If I had twins, I would want identical girls, and I would name them Hope and Grace.)

One last thing. After I hung up on Dad I finished my poem. Here it is:

Summer Storm

In the dark of night,
The still, dark night,
A crash of thunder sounds.
It rocks the city,
The sleeping city,
And through the hills it pounds.

The lightning flares,
Mighty lightning,
And wakes up all the town.
It meets with the earth,
The wet, dark earth.
And tears apart the ground.

Love,
Elizabeth

Date: September 11 10:32.09 PM
From: TSTARR
Subj: WOW!
To: Eliz812

Dear Elizabeth,
I can't believe how calm and how angry you are.

I could never have those two emotions at the same time! I would be yelling and crying and screaming.

Your father is really pond scum. I'm sorry to say that but it's true. (I know you've always said he is "sick" but he's also so selfish . . . and never worries about what you are feeling or how you and your mom and Emma are surviving.)

If he wants some money, he should get a job . . . any job. When Luke had trouble getting jobs, he would take whatever job he could get to support us. You know how he always says, "There are no small jobs . . . only small people." Well, your father should just stop drinking and get a job, and stop calling and torturing you and your family. (I know he never physically hurts you, but it's just terrible what he does emotionally.)

I don't know about not telling your mom. You don't think she would give him money, do you????? What do you think she will do when she finds out? (What will she do with you . . . and with your dad?)

About your poem . . . I really like it. I especially like the use of the word "tears." It's like the earth is ripping apart and like it's causing tears, as in crying. Is that what you meant? Sometimes I'm not sure with poetry. You know I like reading realistic fiction best.

About my life . . . I tried out for the play. I'm sure I won't get the part of Annie. Somehow I don't think I would be good playing a little orphan girl with bad hair. I would much prefer the part of Miss Hannigan, the meanie. It's a really good part, and I don't have to be a "little goody girly." (Remember how we used to call Karen Frank that? Oh, you forgot to mention . . . did she do her traditional first day of school upchuck?)

My twin children are now named . . . Eggbert and Eggsmerelda.

You should hear Luke talk about his "grandchildren." He is so funny. He says he hopes they won't get "spoiled." Barb just sighed when she saw the eggs and said she was hardly old enough to be the mother of a thirteen-year-old, and that she certainly wasn't ready to be a grandmother. Luke hugged her and told her she already was a grand mother, and then he hugged me and patted her stomach. My parents!!!!!!!!

Phil, the twins' father and my husband, seems to be a nice guy. He seems more interested in the assignment than I am. Maybe it's because he's new and doesn't know too many people. Today at lunch I pretended to feed the stupid eggs. Phil burped them.

I didn't even get to sit with Bart at lunch. Lisa said their baby had a bad cold and was "sickly" . . . and so they couldn't sit with other people who would contaminate little Bart Jr. Elizabeth, I'm sure you know how that made me feel. Bart Sr. went along with it. Something tells me it's going to be hard to date him while he's married to Lisa. I really hate this stupid assignment. Why does school have to interfere with my life?

Anyway, I guess that's it for now.

E me soon and tell me what happens when your mom finds out.

I hope your father doesn't call again.

Love,
Tara★

Date: September 15 5:10:39 PM
From: Eliz812
Subj: Pond Scum
To: TSTARR

Dear Tara★,

You're right. My dad is pond scum. You don't have to apologize for calling him that. He's also the scum of the earth. And just generally scummy.

I am in trouble. (Well, I <u>was</u> in trouble.)

I don't remember the last time I was in trouble.

I remember the last time I did something I should have gotten in trouble for — but didn't. It was when I snooped through my parents' things on New Year's Eve and found all those papers that showed me how much financial trouble my father was in. Later I told

Mom what I had done, and we just talked about Dad. No punishment. (Well, I have to admit that I've done a few things since then that I probably should have gotten in trouble for, such as eavesdropping, but Mom didn't find out about them.)

Oh, I know this is all jumbled up, Tara. Let me just tell you what has happened: I read your e-mail last Sunday morning, as soon as I was up. And I started thinking about the questions you had asked — about what Mom would do when she found out about the phone call. I noticed you said <u>when</u> she found out, and this awful feeling crept over me. I just knew that somehow she would find out, even if I didn't tell her. Dad was bound to call back, and I couldn't count on Mom not believing whatever he said. I suspect that these thoughts were really my guilty conscience talking to me. Whatever. I thought and worried all morning, and finally I decided I better tell Mom about the phone call myself. At least I could tell her my side of things before she heard Dad's side. So after lunch, when Emma was on a play date, I asked Mom if I could talk to her. We sat in the living room and I told her everything I could remember from the phone call.

Tara, you are not going to believe the very first thing Mom said when I finished. She said, "Did you hang up before you got his phone number?"

I think I must have stared at her with my mouth open. That was the last thing I would have expected her to say. Actually, it hadn't even occurred to me.

"Yes," I replied.

It was Mom's turn to stare at me. But before she could say anything, I said, "Mom, you've spoken to Dad yourself and <u>you</u> didn't get his number."

After a moment, she said, "That's true." Then she asked why I didn't tell her about the call right away.

I told her I don't want to give Dad any money. I'm mad at him. And I thought the call would upset her.

Mom said she understood. But then she said it was wrong not to give her the message, that I was meddling in someone else's business. I told her I knew it was wrong — I wanted to say, "That's why I'm telling you about the call now," — but I didn't.

So then she told me I was grounded for the rest of the day.

Grounded, Tara! I should never have told her what happened to you over the summer.

Tara, you know what Susie said when I called to cancel our plans for the day? She said Mom is probably angrier than she would be ordinarily because this has to do with Dad. I think Susie is right. And Howie said Mom is probably extra worried at the thought of maybe having to give Dad money right NOW — when she just got the raise and told her parents we don't need financial help from them anymore. Which, I might point out, is precisely why I didn't want to tell Mom about the call in the first place.

Howie wanted to know if Mom goes to Al-Anon meetings. I asked him if he was crazy.

I better sign off. It's time to start dinner, and I am on my best behavior this week. Oh — a few things, though:

> 1. I don't think Dad can "just" stop drinking. I don't think it works like that. I wish he would, but I think that's like saying, "I wish you would just stop having your cold." It takes time to get over a cold — or to stop drinking.

2. He certainly should get a job, though.

3. Karen Frank — she was banned from the drinking fountain all day long, so she barfed on the floor outside the principal's office instead.

4. Love the egg names.

5. I'M SORRY ABOUT BART!!

Love,
Elizabeth

Date: September 18 8:02:25 PM
From: TSTARR
Subj: Reactions, News, and Feelings
To: Eliz812

Dear Elizabeth,

So you got grounded!!!!! Personally, I think it was worth it. It was only for part of a day so it wasn't soooooo terrible . . . and you get to see Howie and Susie all the time anyway. All in all, I don't think that it was too awful. You managed to "hurt" your dad a little (although I do think he's not really aware of how anyone feels but him). You got to let your mother know how you feel (and she is able to be aware . . . and she really cares about you even though she does have her own problems). So grounding was not soooooo bad.

Now for news from Ohio:

1. I GOT THE PART I WANTED IN THE PLAY!!!!!!!!!!!!!! I am Miss Hannigan. I get to be mean to all those little orphans. (Elizabeth, it's just acting!) I get to sing . . . and it doesn't have to be totally on tune either, although I will work on it. (And I love the fact that Lisa, Bart's "wife," tried out for the same part and obviously didn't get it. She will be my understudy. If I get sick, she gets to take my part. . . . Fat chance of that happening. So for now she is working BACKstage. Ha.

2. Speaking of Bart, the other day we went to a party at Hannah's house . . . and you won't believe what happened. Lisa called to tell him there was an emergency . . . that the "baby" was really sick, throwing up, and Bart Sr., had better come over right away.

3. Bart went. He said he had to go because it was important for his grade . . . that Lisa had said she'd tell Mr. Izzard he was being a terrible father if he didn't come right over. I yelled, "It's an egg, a stupid egg. I left my two stupid eggs at home and no one's called to say they're puking."

Elizabeth . . . I am *so* angry. Bart is being hen-pecked and he isn't really even married. (Don't you think henpecked is a funny term, especially for a parent who is the father of a stupid egg?!) Bart said to wait, that he would be back soon, but I called Luke and Barb and they picked me up. I just didn't feel like staying at the party. I know Lisa likes Bart . . . and he must like her. I don't think they did this just for the grade. So my heart is a little broken :-(But not as broken as their egg will be if I get anywhere near it.

Gotta go.

Love,
Tara★

Date: September 21 5:39:49 PM
From: Eliz812
Subj: Boss Lady
To: TSTARR

Dear Tara★,

Well. Whoever thought that being the editor of a poetry magazine could be so . . . nonpoetic. When I came into our office this afternoon (the office of *Silhouette* is a converted broom closet, to give you some idea of its size), I was met with the following:

— two kids whose poems had been rejected, and who wanted to know why.

— a kid who wants to join the staff, even though anyone interested in working on the journal was supposed to have talked to me by last week.

— a kid who's already on the staff, but who wants to take the first month and a half off to be in a community theater production.

— a letter from the editor of the yearbook asking if two afternoons a week their spillover staff can use our equipment.

Luckily (or so I thought) Mrs. Jackson's office is right next to the broom closet, so I ran in there, told Mrs. Jackson everything that was going on, and asked her what I should do. Tara, do you know what she said? She said, "You're the editor, Elizabeth. It's up to you to decide."

Well. I thought being the editor would just mean sitting around reading poems and pasting them up in a nice way with a few illustrations. That's basically what I did last spring when we first started the journal. I guess it's grown since then. And I guess I didn't realize quite how much work Mrs. Jackson was doing for us.

I went back to the journal office and looked at all the kids standing there. I told them they would need to schedule appointments to see me later in the week. (Personally, I am leaning toward telling the theater kid she can just drop out and letting the new kid take her place. Don't you think there's some POETIC JUS-TICE to that?)

I am a little crabby, Tara. Or at least I was after everyone had left. Howie and Susie showed up a while later, and when I told them what had happened, we ended up working out how to handle everything. I'm going to sit down with the first two kids individually (the ones who want to know why their poems were rejected), and go over the poems line by line with them. Then I'll invite them to resubmit the poems after they edit them, or to submit other poems — but I'll tell them I can't promise that the new poems will be published either. . . .

Well, I won't go into all the details about the other problems, but I feel much better now. And — I have to admit it — kind of proud of myself for actually handling the problems, even if I did get help from Howie and Susie.

Tara, I feel awful about Bart and Lisa. (Has it occurred to you that Bart and Lisa are the siblings in *The Simpsons?* And that Bart Simpson is basically a jerk?)

Oh, I almost forgot the most important thing: CON-GRATULATIONS on getting the part of Miss Hannigan!

That is so cool! The only bad thing is that I feel just like I did last year when you got the part in *Cheaper by the Dozen* and I realized I wouldn't get to see you in it. Is this how our friendship is always going to be? If so, I don't like it! But you are going to have so much fun. I know *Annie* practically by heart. You get to sing really good songs. "Little Girls" and "Easy Street" are two of my favorites from the whole show. Also, I think you get to sit in a rocker and sing a song from an old Jell-O commercial, which is pretty funny.

I better go now. Mom and Emma will be home any minute, so I should finish getting supper ready.

No more word from Dad (that I know of).

Love,
Elizabeth

P.S. Howie told me this afternoon that he's thinking of putting a plaque up just outside the principal's office. It will read KAREN FRANK BARF MEMORIAL.

Date: September 22 7:30:57 PM
From: TSTARR
Subj: I love bad puns and this one is bad
To: Eliz812

Mahatma Gandhi walked barefoot everywhere. Eventually his feet became quite thick and hard. He was also a very spiritual person. Even when he was not on a hunger strike, he did not eat much and became quite thin and frail. Furthermore, due to his diet, he wound up with very gross, very bad breath. THEREFORE: He came to be known as a "super calloused fragile mystic plagued with halitosis."

Elizabeth . . . don't you just love this joke?????????? A kid in my homeroom sent it to me on a note and I wanted to share it with you ASAP.

I just love e-mail, don't you????? It means we can keep in touch much faster.

However, I don't have time to write tonight. I've got a stupid math test to study for. And I have to do some journal writing about Eggbert and Eggsmerelda. I think I will say that today they were so bad that if they don't improve I'm going to send them to the penitentiary, where they are going to get "fried."

Love,
Tara★

Date: September 23 7:30:36 PM
From: TSTARR
Subj: Whatta Day!
To: Eliz812

Zounds. Gadzooks. Cablooey. (I just made that one up to try to explain my day.)

So much has happened that I hardly know where to start. . . .

Bart and I had a big BIG fight in the cafeteria. Actually, I was the one who yelled . . . and OK, who poured the milk on top of his head. And he just sat there. For someone so smart, I can't believe he can be so stupid.

He said that Lisa had said their baby was having trouble understanding why he was spending so much time with me. (Bart and I made up after the party.) She said the baby was crying a lot and asking for his daddy and that, for the assignment, it was important for them to spend more time together as a family. She said Mr. Izzard had stated that they were a family "at a crossroads" and their assignment was to try to work things out. I swear, Elizabeth, this is just the dumbest thing. They are, as I have said numerous times before and will continue to say, STUPID EGGS . . . and the relationship that Bart should be concerned about is ours. (Okay, so it's only a seventh-grade thing, but it should mean something.) But Bart worries about his grades and what his parents will say if he doesn't get all A's. (They are always reminding him that he has to work hard to get into the college of his choice. Ha! I know it will be the college of *their* choice.) So Bart asked me if we could just not see each other until the project ended. I gave him his answer by pouring the milk on his head. I hadn't planned on doing that.

People at our table applauded. I took a bow.

Bart left to sit with Lisa and their baby. I hope the baby never gets the grades to go to the college of his choice, that he turns out to be "a bad egg."

As for my twin bundles of egghood, they seem to be doing fine. Phil is coming over to my house this weekend, so we can work on the assignment together. (I know what you are thinking. . . . Phil is Tara★'s next boyfriend. But oh no, he's just becoming a friend. And anyway, I've sworn off boys for now.)

You are NOT going to believe this next thing. I don't know what's happening with Luke and Barb. They are getting so gooey about the new baby . . . and about me . . . and about being a family. The other day Barb even said, "The three of us always just sort of seemed like three people hanging out. Four is going to be a family." Yes, that is what she said. I personally always thought we were a family, but there you go. Anyway, they went out for a walk together. (Or a "waddle" as Barb likes to say.) And they came back with a kitten. . . . A KITTEN. Do you believe it? And not just a guest kitten . . . a kitten to stay. Yikes. A neighbor convinced them that this was just what was needed. Now I have a litter pan to trip over in the kitchen. It's so attractive and I am sure it will really add something to the kitchen aromas.

I'm doing so much. There's the column. (This month it is an editorial about the use of frogs in biology classes.

I called it "A Frog in Your Throat.") Hannah and I have started a reading group. The first book is *A Separate Peace*. Maybe you would like to read it "with" us. Probably, though, you will want to read it with Howie and Susie . . . the "ie's" I call them — as in the "E's" . . . Howeeeeee and Suseeeeee). And I've got the play.

I am having so much fun . . . and it's just started.

I can tell that you are very busy too. It sounds like being editor of the poetry magazine is hard work. You have soooooo many decisions to make, so much to do to keep it all going. Will you have time to write your own poetry?

I can't blame you for feeling crabby.

I thought Howie's idea of putting up a plaque outside the principal's office to commemorate Karen Frank's barfing was a very good idea. However, I would like to suggest decorating it with one of those gargoyle faces with liquid coming out of its mouth.

Enough already. I've got to get back to work.

Love,
Tara ★

Date: September 23 8:48:21 PM
From: Eliz812
Subj:KITTENS!!!
To: TSTARR

Dear Tara★,

I almost never look at my e-mail twice in one day. I
don't know what possessed me to turn on the computer tonight while Mom was putting Emma to bed,
but I am sooooooo glad I did. . . .

A KITTEN?! I CAN'T BELIEVE YOU HAVE A KITTEN!
YOU ARE SO LUCKY! CONGRATULATIONS!!!!!!!

I have always wanted a kitten. Or a cat. I wouldn't be
picky about its age, but a kitten looks like so much
fun. I would name my kitten Tippy. Or possibly
Buster — as in Buster Kitten. Wouldn't that be cute?
Of course, I suppose you should actually see a kitten
and get to know it a little before you settle on a name
for it. What color is your kitten? Or what colors?

Hey, you didn't say whether it's a boy or a girl. I've heard that male cats are more affectionate, but I don't know. Tell me everything about the kitten. Have you let it sleep in your bed with you yet? If not, where does it sleep? Where did the neighbor get the kitten? Was it a stray? Do you have a rescue kitten? Does it have brothers and sisters? You might want to consider getting just one more kitten so your kitten won't get lonely.

The joke: Ha-ha. A very good pun.

Tara, about Howie and Susie. You sounded just a teeny bit jealous of them in your last e. And, well, in fact, you have already said you are jealous that I have new friends. And I understand that and think it's kind of sweet, but I do have to point out that you too have new friends. You have quite a few of them. Actually, you have way more of them than I do. And you do want me to have friends, don't you? I mean, you wouldn't really want me to have you as my only friend, especially when I can hardly ever see you. Would you? Don't you want me to have friends I can see every day? Talk to? Hang out with? (Just like you do.) Remember last year when things had gotten horrible with my father and I had only you to turn to? You said that put too much pressure on you.

About Bart. He must be an even bigger jerk than I thought. I'm so sorry about what happened. (But glad about the milk incident.) Phil sounds nice, though, and I'm glad you and he are going to be friends.

It's getting late (for me) and I still have a little home-work to finish. Plus, I'm in the middle of a poem. (Yes, I still make time for my own poetry.) I'm writ-ing one now about autumn leaves.

I really like the idea of your book club, and I MIGHT read the books along with you and Hannah, but I'm not sure how much time I'll have. I think I'm busy enough with homework, my dinner responsibilities, baby-sitting for Emma on weekends (sometimes), and the poetry journal. Howie and Susie and I don't even have Poetry Night anymore. We were only able to do that in the summer.

Okay. I better go.

Love,
Elizabeth

P.S. Kiss the kitten for me.

Date: September 26 10:00:51 PM
From: TSTARR
Subj: Ramblings and Rantings
To: Eliz812

Dear Elizabeth,

The kitten's name is Little Bo. Luke and Barb said I should name it, so I did. (I think they wanted me to name it so I won't feel left out when they name my Future Sibling. We know they don't trust me with that job!!!!) Its real name is Little Bo Poop, but I didn't mention that to my parents.

I think they seriously expect me to bond with the critter. Don't they realize I already have enough responsibility with the eggoids? Elizabeth, I realize that you would get all goopy and gushy if you saw Little Bo. It's black and orange. It has four paws, two eyes, a little nose, and a very rough tongue. At least they didn't bring home a puppy that would need to be walked.

About the name . . . I decided on it after having to deal with the litter pan, which you will be glad to know has been moved out of the kitchen and into the bathroom. You can only imagine my happiness on getting out of the shower and stepping on kitty litter that has escaped from the pan. Lovely. And Little Bo Poop lives up to its name. . . .

Oh, I don't know what sex it is. I really didn't care to look.

Eggbert and Eggsmerelda continue to exist. I haven't dropped them yet. In fact, I made Eggsmerelda the cutest little outfit the other day. Two sequins now cover what would be her chest if she had one . . . and I've put a little grass skirt around what I assume is her waist. I'm still thinking about what Eggbert should wear. Phil says that whatever I make will be fine as long as Eggbert doesn't end up with egg on his face.

About Howie and Susie . . . You are right. I am "just a teeny bit jealous of them." Actually, more than a teeny bit jealous. I do understand, though. Of course I want you to have friends. I'm happy that you have friends. In fact, I'm relieved that you have friends. I just hate getting all your news after Howie and Susie do. . . . I hate that you turn to them first for advice. I know this isn't logical . . . or right. But I feel that way. And you know something, Elizabeth? I like them. I think they are really nice people and TRULY, I am glad they are your friends. I just don't like the fact that you might like them more than you like me. This is not rational. . . . I know that. I do have friends here, and they do hear about stuff before you do. And I do ask Hannah for advice before I ask you. So I shouldn't be jealous. But I am. Sigh. It's just another thing for me to work on as I go through life's journey.

Elizabeth . . . you are not going to believe what happened just now. Luke walked in with Little Bo and introduced it to the stupid eggs. Before he left, he said that Little Bo is their aunt. Where is the Karen Frank Barfola Memorial when I need it???????!!!!!!!!???????!!!!!!

Aaarg. Little Bo is trying to bat Eggbert and Eggsmerelda with its paw. . . . Let me "paws" now while writing this e-mail to rescue my little darlings. Do you know that this project will count for 40 percent of my grade this marking period? If Little Bo breaks them . . . the yoke is on me.

Bye for now.

TSTARR

Date: September 27 3:49:02 PM
From: Eliz812
Subj: Little Bo
To: TSTARR

Dear Tara★,

I just got home from school and checked my e-mail
first thing. And I'm writing back to you immediately
because I have to tell you something important. It
occurs to me that if you really don't know what sex
Little Bo is (and by the way, I love the name!), that
means you haven't taken the kitten to the vet yet.
Tara, you do know that you should take it to the vet
right away, don't you? All kittens and cats have to be
checked for certain diseases, like feline leukemia and
feline AIDS. If they test positive, then they have to
be kept away from other cats FOREVER because they
are contagious (but only to other cats). If they test

negative, then they should get shots to protect them from those diseases. Plus, the vet should check Little Bo for worms and ear mites and stuff. And weigh him/her. And of course tell you what sex it is. And tell you what kind of food is best for Little Bo and how much it should be eating, and how old Little Bo should be before you have him/her neutered. Also, did you know that Barb should NOT change Little Bo's litter box while she's pregnant? It isn't safe for her. You and Luke will have to do that fun job.

Okay, I really have to run. I have to get over to Howie's. Then get back here and fix dinner.

More some other time.

Love,
Elizabeth

Date: September 27 5:31:44 PM
From: Eliz812
Subj: Friends
To: TSTARR

Dear Tara★,

Okay. Now I have a little more time. Just about half an hour before Mom and Emma come home.

Tara, I know this is just my reaction to what you said in your last e, and it may not be any more rational than some of the things you told me about our friendship, but I have to say it. I'm glad you like Howie and Susie, I'm glad you're happy and relieved that I have friends, but it truly annoys me when I hear you say that you ask Hannah for advice before you ask me — yet you "hate" that I turn to Howie and Susie first for advice. I know you know you shouldn't be jealous, that you say this is something you have to work on, but I find it really annoying. I think because it's so unfair. Maybe I should work on being less annoyed, but as you have said, a person can't help the way she feels. And this is how I feel.

Another thing. Don't expect everyone to like you the best of all. You're going to be disappointed. I don't expect everyone I know to like me the best. Plus, some of the people I know also know you. Should I expect our mutual friends to like Tara Starr Lane the best of all the people they know? That seems a bit unfair too.

Anyway, I'm not mad at you, Tara; just annoyed by a couple of things you said. Which I do recognize is my problem, not yours. But I wanted to tell you how I feel.

I know this e might make you mad, but I'm going to risk that. You're still one of my best friends. (Remember when you said the same thing to me last year?!) But you are, of course. I don't think anything will change that.

Lots of Love,
Elizabeth

P.S. Tell me when you take Little Bo to the vet. I want to know whether you have a boy or a girl.

Date: September 29 7:04:11 PM
From: TSTARR
Subj: A Can of Worms . . . Actually, Two Cans of Worms
To: Eliz812

I wonder where that phrase came from — "You're opening a can of worms"???????????? — Any ideas? Just wondering!

Anyway — Can of Worms #1: Little Bo

Barb and Luke got the kitten from a lady down the street, who said, "Don't forget. Take it to the vet." But none of us thought it was that important. We figured we could wait . . . or even do nothing since our family health insurance doesn't cover cats. It's good you told us about all the things that can happen if you don't take care of kittens, and also about Barb not handling the litter box. So, a gazillion dollars later, we know we have an almost perfectly healthy pet. (See . . . I'm even calling Little Bo a pet, not just "it.") He's fine and he got his shots. That's right, HE. . . . Little Bo is a boy. (I think Luke is kind of hoping this is an omen that the baby will be a boy too. Barb and I told him that now there are two males and two females in the house, and the baby will be the tiebreaker in the competition of boy-girl numbers.) I'm happy to report that Little Bo doesn't have ear mites. He does have worms, though (gross). We just have to give him a couple of pills and they will be all gone. So now you don't have to worry. Our cat is practically purrfect!

Can of Worms #2: Friends

I feel like saying "lighten up." I'm sorry you find it really annoying when I mention things that even I admit are flaws. . . . I do admit that it isn't rational to feel the way I do sometimes, but my way of working some things out is to say them out loud. I think that's an open, honest thing to do.

You know, Elizabeth, I've figured something out. It's not just that I feel JEALOUS that you turn to Howie and Susie first. It's also that I realize we *both* turn to other people first and that makes me think about how differ-ent our friendship is . . . and *that* makes me a little SAD. (It's not your fault or anything. We both turn to others first now, which makes our e-mails sound more like re-ports than like talking, or like the way we used to talk.) This isn't a BAD difference, but it's VERY different. We have other friends, other interests. You're changing, I'm changing, our friendship is changing.

Elizabeth . . . do you think that even if I hadn't moved we would have stayed best friends, or even "one of our best friends"????? It's just a thought.

As for my expecting everyone to like me best, I didn't say that. I said specifically that you might like Howie and Susie better than me, and that would bother me. That's different than expecting the whole world to like me best. (Although I wouldn't mind that . . . joke.)

Well, now we both know how we feel . . . and that's good, I think. Don't you think so too?

Anyway, I've got to go now. Little Bo, Eggbert, and Eggsmerelda are all demanding attention. Little Bo is purring and rubbing himself against my leg. The eggoids need to be read to (class assignment). Tonight I'm reading *Squids Will Be Squids*. I hope they think it is as funny as I do. (I don't think they liked the book Phil and I read to them at school yesterday — *Green Eggs and Ham*.)

And if that isn't enough, I have to continue memorizing the script . . . and I have more homework to do!!!!!!!!!!

Yikes. . . . Did I tell you Bart and Lisa are reading *Moby Dick* to their egg? It's enough to make me whale . . . I mean wail.

Lots of love to you too.
Tara★

Date: October 3 11:49:28 AM
From: Eliz812
Subj: Dad again
To: TSTARR

Dear Tara★,

I was going to write back to you much earlier, and I was going to start my letter by pointing out that despite whatever you may think about me, sometimes I too try to work things out by saying them out loud. (You're not the only one.) And yes, it's an open, honest thing to do — which was why I was doing it in my last letter to you. You tell me I keep too many things to myself. Then I open up and tell you something honest . . . and you (almost) tell me to lighten up. Hmm. There's something hypocritical going on here.

Anyway, the reason I didn't write back right away was that a few days ago, just when I was <u>about</u> to write to you, our doorbell rang. It was a little after 4:00 in the afternoon and I was the only one home. I looked through our peephole and saw the UPS delivery woman. She had this enormous package. We weren't expecting anything, but the package was addressed to Emma, so I accepted it and managed to wrestle it inside. A package for Emma? Weird. I examined it and found a return address. It was from . . . Dad. The address was South Bergenfield, NJ. Is that his new home address? If so, he isn't very far away.

Anyway, I didn't know what to do about the package, Tara. I didn't want Emma to see it right away, because she gets so upset about Dad, and I needed to know how Mom wanted to handle the situation. Now, our apartment is on the small side, to say the least, and there was no room to hide such a large box. So I lugged the package over to Howie's and he said I could leave it on his patio for a while. When Mom came home, I talked to her privately and told her about the box. She said I did the right thing by not letting Emma see it. And after dinner we asked Susie to baby-sit for Emma while Mom and I went to Howie's to look in the box.

Oh, Tara, it was so embarrassing . . . having to explain to Howie's father about MY stupid father. But

Mr. Besser was really understanding. And he left Mom and me alone on the patio while we opened the box.

If we were talking on the phone now, this is the point at which I would say, "I'll give you ten guesses about what was in the box." Then you would guess ten things, starting with really weird items and then taking the game more and more seriously, and I can guarantee that no matter what, you would not be able to guess what was in that box.

Dad had sent Emma, a five-year-old, her very own stereo. No wonder the box was so big and heavy. The stereo came with speakers and everything. Now I ask you . . . WHY????? And where did he get the $$ for such a thing? It's really expensive, and really, really inappropriate. We don't have room for it, and Emma doesn't want or need a stereo (her Minnie Mouse cassette player is just fine for her Barney tapes).

I watched Mom's face as we opened the box and realized what was inside. First she looked puzzled, then annoyed, then as if she were going to cry.

Mom took a moment to collect herself. Then we went inside the Bessers' apartment and Mr. Besser made coffee for himself and Mom. Mom actually talked with him about what to do about the stupid present!

In the end, Mom and Mr. Besser talked for about an hour, while Howie and I worked on some *Silhouette* stuff. The next day, Mom shipped the box back to Dad.

Now we know where he lives, Tara. (Or at least we think we do. Maybe he uses somebody else's address.) Isn't that weird? And we haven't heard from him even though we're pretty sure he's gotten the box back by now.

As Alice would say, things are getting "curiouser and curiouser."

I'm glad to hear about Little Bo, and about Eggbert and Eggsmerelda.

And I do agree that it's sad our friendship is changing. Not bad. Just sad.

You're STILL one of my best friends, though.

Love,
Elizabeth

Date: October 7 8:09:50 PM
From: TSTARR
Subj: So many things, so little time
To: Eliz812

I am dumbfounded by what your father has done. (Not to digress, but who ever invented the word dumbfounded? Who would found a dumb?!!!!) Anyway, I am dumbfounded and SHOCKED by your father's latest action. He's called to ask your mother for money and then he spends a lot on something that is soooooo unnecessary. He should probably be spending the money on getting his head examined.

Elizabeth, you were sooooo smart to lug the package over to Howie's. And it sounds like Mr. Besser was really wonderful and helpful. (Didn't you say he's a widower? Hmmmmmmm. Do you think he and your mom might ever . . . ? Hmmmmmmmm.)

It sounds like you are handling everything well.

As for me . . .

The only boy in my life right now is Little Bo. We are actually sleeping together. As males go, I guess he's a good CATch. Ho-ho. Anyway, yes, I am beginning to love my kitten.

As for my eggs (my children, as Mr. Izzard says), they are still fine. At least I think they are. Phil's got custody for a couple of days, since I am so busy with the play.

Oh, Elizabeth . . . the play is so much fun. I've got almost all of my lines learned, my songs are going well, and . . . it's all just so much fun!

The other night I went to a party, without a date, and I had a great time. (Bart and Lisa were not invited! I think they stayed "home" and watched their little darling.)

Speaking of Bart, he came up to me during lunch today and said he missed me and that once the assignment was over, he wants us to get back together again. And then he just stood there looking very cute. I had to think about it . . . but only for a millisecond . . . and then I said, "Thanks but no thanks." I'm learning that I am fine without a boyfriend and that rather than being with someone just to be with someone, I can be OK alone. (Well, OK . . . alone . . . but with lots of friends).

Anyway, I'm going to stop writing now. Barb came home early from work today. (She's done that a couple of times lately. Can you believe she's SEVEN months pregnant??????) She's resting, so I'm going to do the dishes.

Love from one of your best friends,
Tara★

Date: October 10 7:46:13 PM
From: Eliz812
Subj: News of the Week
To: TSTARR

Dear Tara★,

What a week. Everything is just so . . . all over the place. I guess you never know what to expect. Remember that letter from the yearbook editor? The one asking if her staff could use the *Silhouette* equipment sometimes? Well, it really was not the most convenient thing, so I spent about three hours working on a letter back to her, but even so, I kind of expected that the yearbook advisor would talk to Mrs. Jackson and we'd wind up having to share our equipment anyway. But that didn't happen. Sharon Meigs — she's the editor — wrote back to <u>me</u> and said she completely understands, and she's going to try to work out something with the computer lab, which makes much more sense anyway. So one problem turned out not to be a problem at all.

But then (and this is <u>so</u> not good) it turns out that Emma's after-school day-care center is going to close on December 31st. Mom is going crazy. What are we going to do with Emma every day after kindergarten? We can't afford the other day-care centers in town, Mom <u>has</u> to work (and she can't bring Emma with her), and even I can't watch Emma because kindergarten ends a couple of hours before I get out of school. Mom has been really upset by this. I think it's because when something like this throws us into such a tailspin it reminds Mom how precarious our lives are. On the surface, everything seems great. But really it's a balancing act. Mom is making JUST enough $$ to support us. And she's worked out her schedule (and Emma's and mine) so that it's JUST barely manageable. But one little change, and poof, we have a BIG problem. So Mom is frantic. We have to get Emma some kind of day care (that Mom can afford) in the next few months.

And then of course there's my father. Yeah, he definitely needs his head examined. (If I really thought he'd do it, I'd lend him the $$ for it.) I keep thinking about when he called and asked to borrow $$. Was it so he could buy the stereo for Emma? But why would he want do to that? I mean, why would he get it into his head to buy Emma a stereo? Why buy her a gift at all? It's not her birthday. And why buy her such an expensive stereo?

You know what I thought of last night, Tara? (This thought jolted me right out of sleep.) WHAT IF THE STEREO WAS STOLEN? Even worse, WHAT IF DAD STOLE IT? I can't quite see him doing that, but then, six months ago, if you'd asked me if Dad could leave our family, I would have said no.

We still haven't heard from Dad. Mom was sure we would after we sent the box back. She tried to get a phone number for Dad at the address that was on the box, but the operator couldn't find anything listed for him anywhere. I told Mom she should just drive to South Bergenfield and try to find the address, but she doesn't want to. It's so weird. She keeps expecting him to return to our lives, but she doesn't want to go after him herself. I'll have to think about what that means.

About Mom and Mr. Besser . . . You know what? I was thinking just what you're thinking. Mr. Besser is

<u>so</u> nice. It figures, since Howie is so nice (and cute). I was kind of hoping Mr. Besser might call Mom after the night we opened the box on their patio. But he hasn't. And Mom hasn't called him (that I know of). On the other hand, Howie and I went to the movies last night. Just the two of us. We sat in the back row, and our hands almost touched. In fact, they were so close that I could feel the HEAT from his hand. It was nice.

Say hi to the Egg Twins for me, kiss Little Bo on his nose, and give my love to Barb and Luke. . . . Seven months. That is so hard to believe. Here's what I'm planning to make for the baby — a reversible flannel receiving blanket. What do you think?

Love,
Elizabeth

Date: October 13 6:02:45 PM
From: TSTARR
Subj: A Fast Note
To: Eliz812

Dear Elizabeth,

I've got to get ready. . . . Phil is on his way over with the "kids." Our assignment tonight is to budget our money to provide for college educations for the little critters. We also have to talk about our philosophies about child rearing (actually, egg rearing, but what the heck). We have to turn in a "philosophy" paper tomorrow. Yikes.

I'm a little excited that Phil is coming over. He really is one of the nicest guys I've ever met. I'm getting to know him and I really like him. That doesn't mean he's going to be a boyfriend (well, maybe, but I don't want to rush into anything this time). Anyway, it's fun working with him . . . and funny. Yesterday we spent twenty minutes trying to decide which egg looked like each of us. He said Eggsmerelda had my smile. (It's a good thing he didn't say she had my bust, since hers are just two sequins.)

Enough silliness. Now on to serious stuff. What are you going to do about Emma?????? Can your grandparents help out and send her back to Miss Fine's????? Are there other parents who have kids at that day-care center who can help find a solution??? Why did the day-care center close? (Just curious.)

About your mom looking for your dad . . . Yuck.

About your mom and Mr. Besser . . . That has definite possibilities! I think you and Howie should plot a way to get them together, but then if they did get together that would be kind of weird if you and Howie also became a couple . . . kind of like a weird Brady Bunch. (I know. . . . Don't go there.)

Now, about you and Howie . . . the movies, hmm . . . and your hands almost touched . . . so close you could feel the heat from his hand . . . and it was nice. Hmmmmmmmmm. The plot thickens. I can't wait for the next episode.

I have said hello to the Egg Twins for you. (They say, "Hi, Aunt Elizabeth. You are definitely a good egg.") I tried to kiss Little Bo on his nose for you, but he licked me on my mouth. (I have limits!) Also, I've given your love to Luke and Barb. (They send their love back.) And I think that the baby will love a reversible flannel receiving blanket. What is a receiving blanket? Does that mean the baby will receive the blanket . . . or is that a sports term??? I'm very confused. Is this something that the Egg Twins will need?

Gotta go. Phil is here.

Love,
Tara★

Date: October 21 5:19:50 PM
From: Eliz812
Subj: Receiving Blankets
To: TSTARR

Dear Tara★,

I'm sorry I haven't written in so long, but I wanted to wait until you got the package before I wrote again. Did you get it yet? I hope you got it. Maybe it just arrived today. So . . . how do you like what's inside? In case you can't tell what they are, they are little mini receiving blankets for Eggbert and Eggsmerelda made by me, their aunt Elizabeth. Now you can see what a receiving blanket is. Although I'm still not sure why it's called that. I looked up "receiving blanket" in the dictionary and it said "A small, lightweight blanket, usually made of cotton, for wrapping a baby in." But why is it called a <u>receiving</u> blanket? Is it because you're supposed to wrap a baby in it when he receives his visitors? And since my blankets are made of flannel, do they still qualify as receiving blankets? Well, in any case, now you can see what I am going to make for your little brother or sister. By the way, do you like the egg theme on Eggbert's and Eggsmerelda's blankets? Humpty Dumpty, chicks hatching out of eggs . . . it's amazing how many fabrics you can find at Jo-Beth's.

Well, back to serious stuff.

Emma's day-care center is going to close because of lack of funding. Most of the parents (like Mom) who send their kids there can't afford to pay much. And there's less and less government funding now for places like the day-care center. The parents tried to raise $$ themselves, but they just couldn't raise enough. They're all working at full-time jobs and raising families, and they don't have time for a lot of fund-raising on top of everything else. Anyway, there is simply no $$ left. I don't know what the other parents are going to do, but I know Mom's been talking with them. We'll come up with something, I'm sure. Mom doesn't want to ask Nana and Grandpa for help again, but I guess she will if she has to. (Miss Fine's, by the way, is just a preschool. Emma's too old for it now. It only had morning classes anyway.)

Still no word from Dad.

BUT . . . (And this is such a big but, so to speak, that I nearly broke down and wrote to you about it last weekend before the package arrived) . . . BUT . . . MR. BESSER CALLED MOM. Neither Howie nor I knew that was going to happen. The phone rang last Friday evening and I answered it and it was Mr. Besser, asking to talk to Mom. Naturally, I tried to overhear as much of Mom's end of the conversation as possible. I couldn't catch every single word, but I caught enough to know that Mr. Besser was inviting Mom to go out for coffee sometime. (What is it with adults and coffee?) I was wild with excitement, and all I wanted to do was call Howie and ask him if he knew what was going on, but of course I couldn't because Mom was still on the phone. When she finally hung up I didn't know what to do first: ask her what Mr. Besser wanted (like I didn't know), call Howie, call Susie, or send you an e.

Before I could make up my mind, Mom said to me, "Well, that was interesting." I think she was trying to look puzzled, but instead she looked pleased, and a little flustered. Her cheeks were pink and she was patting at her hair.

"What?" I said.

"Well, Stu and I are going to go out for coffee tomorrow afternoon."

STU, Tara! She called him Stu!

Anyway, the coffee date happened last Saturday. I think it went well. Howie and I considered spying on Mom and Stu from Dunkin' Donuts, which is across the street, but in the end we decided to be mature adults and we spent an hour at Chuck E. Cheese instead. (We gave all our prizes to Emma.)

About Howie and me. I STILL don't know exactly what we are. I mean, are we just really, really close friends? Well, we are, but is there more to it? I don't know. Like I said, our hands didn't even touch. And I felt the heat from Howie and thought it was nice, but did he feel any heat from me? Did he feel anything? And come to think of it, I thought the heat was nice, but . . . that's all. This was not a moment you could make a movie about.

So . . . you and Phil? Anything new? How did your philosophy paper turn out? How is Little Bo? Your mom? Bad Bart? Keep me posted.

Love,
Elizabeth

Date: October 18 10:06:59 PM
From: TSTARR
Subj: Trouble
To: Eliz812

Dear Elizabeth,
I'm sorry I haven't been in touch, but a lot has been happening . . . and not a lot of it good.

1. There's a chance something bad might happen to the baby. Barb went into premature labor last week and the doctor wants her to stay in bed until she has the baby. Dr. Yancy said she could stay in bed at home, and that's what Barb wants to do. (Hospital expenses . . . and Barb's not crazy about hospitals anyway.) So Barb has taken a leave from her job and is at home . . . in bed. She can't get up much at all.

2. Luke said he would drop out of school to take care of her . . . but Barb said absolutely not.

3. So . . . she has some friends checking in on her during the day, and I come home immediately after school.

4. That's right . . . immediately after school, which means I have dropped out of the play (and Lisa now has my part!).

5. Elizabeth . . . it was my choice. Nobody made me do it. It's better that Luke stay in school and keep earning money, and I'll have other chances to be in a play.

6. It's very scary. I don't want anything bad to happen to my mom. I'm afraid something awful will happen to her . . . and to the baby.

7. I was getting used to the thought of the baby and had actually begun to think of her as my little sister. (No . . . we don't know what sex the baby is, but I am positive she is a girl.)

8. I hope the baby isn't premature. My friend Becca said her little sister was premature and had to spend a long time in an incubator. If that

has to happen, OK . . . as long as the baby is all right. Becca's sister is fine . . . bratty but fine. I hope the baby can just wait until she is strong enough to make it on her own.

I've got to go now. Phil is on his way over with the eggs. It's so weird to have to do that . . . deal with stupid fragile eggs when something this big is happening to a real baby.

You know, Bart and Lisa's egg fell and broke the other day . . . and I actually feel bad about it.

I feel a little numb right now.

I'll write when I can.

Love,
TSTARR

October 19 4:14:29 PM
INSTANT MESSAGE

Eliz812: Hi, Tara! I see your name on my Buddy List, I just got your e from last night and wanted to chat. Do you have a minute?

THE MEMBER YOU ARE TRYING TO REACH IS NOT CURRENTLY AVAILABLE.

October 29 4:14:42 PM
INSTANT MESSAGE

Eliz812: Tara? Your name is still on my Buddy List, but it's in parentheses. Maybe that means you're using the computer but you can't get this message for some reason. I'm trying one more time. Are you there? Here's our chance to "talk." Please, please answer this if you get it.

THE MEMBER YOU ARE TRYING TO REACH IS NOT CURRENTLY AVAILABLE.

October 29 9:41:48 PM
INSTANT MESSAGE

Eliz812: Tara, it's me again. I'll stay on the computer for a while in case you want to try to send me an IM.

THE MEMBER YOU ARE TRYING TO REACH IS NOT CURRENTLY AVAILABLE.

Date: October 30 11:24:11 PM
From: Eliz812
Subj: THE BABY
To: TSTARR

Dear Tara★,

I tried all yesterday afternoon and evening to send you Instant Messages, which I guess you're not receiving for some reason. Ever since I got your last e I've been wanting to "talk" with you.

Anyway, I can't believe your e. I feel horrible about the baby, the play, even Bart's egg . . . but especially about the baby. How is Barb feeling now? Any changes? Anything different? Anything I should know about?

Tara, I think you did the right thing when you decided to take care of Barb in the afternoons. It's like when I told Mom I would get home in time to make dinner every night. I sort of figure it's the least I can do. I mean, these are our families, right? What else would we do but pitch in and help?

So what happened when Barb went into premature labor? (You don't have to answer that if you don't want to.) Was it scary? Did she have to go to the hospital? Did you go with her?

I just figured out that if Barb really does have to stay in bed until her due date, that's almost two MONTHS. What a long time, I hope she has plenty of books to read. I hope she isn't bored already.

You said she can't get up much. Can she get up to go to the bathroom? Does she have to eat her meals in bed? What happens when she has a doctor's appointment? Does the doctor make house calls?

And Tara, the play. That's awful. I do think you're doing the right thing, but it's still awful. You must be so disappointed. Will you go see the play with Lisa in it? I bet you will, just to be grown-up. But I bet Lisa won't be nearly as good a Miss Hannigan as you would have been.

What about your column for the paper? I guess you can work on that at home. And obviously Phil can come over with the eggs, so that isn't a problem. What about the yearbook? Can you work on that at home too?

Well, to change the subject . . . I was just thinking of something weird. Today is the day before Halloween. I remember writing you a letter last year around Halloween, or maybe on Halloween. It was such a bad time. I didn't know what was going on with Dad yet, but we were all anxious. And I didn't have any friends (I mean, any friends here) and didn't want to have any friends. Now it's a year later — and SO different. Dad is gone, so family things are better, and I have Howie and Susie. Susie and I have been busy making costumes for Matt and Emma. Tomorrow afternoon we'll take the kids trick-or-treating in DEER RUN (they should really rake in the candy, since so many people live here, plus with Halloween on Sunday most everyone should be at home). And tonight, Howie and Susie and I are going to a Halloween party/dance at school. I'd like to be able to tell you that Howie is my date, but the three of us are going together, as a group. Howie will be the Tin Man from *The Wizard of Oz,* Susie will be the Scarecrow, and I am going to be Dorothy. I'm even going to carry a basket with a stuffed dog in it. The only stuffed dog Emma has that will fit in the basket is a dalmatian, but that's okay. (By the way, Emma's costume is a princess, and Matt's is a fireman. That is SO five years old.)

Are you doing anything tonight or tomorrow, Tara? Party? Dance? Trick-or-treating? Or do you have to stay at home? If you do, maybe Phil could come over and you could make costumes for Eggbert, Eggsmerelda, and Little Bo.

Speaking of Little Bo, how is he? How are his worms?

Hey, you didn't say whether you received the receiving blankets. (I know you could make a pun out of that, but I can't.)

Write when you have a chance.

Give Barb and Luke and the baby my love,
Elizabeth

Date: November 2 7:02:18 PM
From: TSTARR
Subj: The Three B's . . . the Baby, Barb, and Bored
To: Eliz812

The report (it's easier putting it in a list):

1. What happened . . . Barb was making dinner (Luke was at work with the car), and she went into premature labor and started to bleed. We called 911 and an ambulance came and took her (us) to the hospital. It was very scary. When we got to the hospital, her doctor was already there (had just delivered a baby). She examined Barb and said she had to stay in the hospital overnight. Luke arrived (I'd called him from the hospital) and he took me home and then went back to the hospital. Around midnight he came home and said that everything seemed OK . . . that the baby

hadn't miscarried or come too early. (I *would* have a sibling who wants to rush into the world!!!!!) Elizabeth, I was so scared waiting alone in the apartment, not knowing what was happening with Barb and the baby.

2. The doctor explained everything to me when I called her. (Barb had said I should call the doctor so I wouldn't worry that my parents were keeping something from me.) The doc says that if the baby arrived now and was alive, it could end up in neonatal intensive care until her birthday (the baby's estimated birth day, not the doctor's birthday). It would eventually have to be at least five pounds to get out with no need for life support.

3. Barb must stay in bed or on the couch . . . no cooking, no cleaning, no anything having to do with housework. (That's my job for now. Luke helps out a little bit but not much because he is trying to stay in school and go to work.) Thankfully, Barb can go to the bathroom on her own.

4. I am bored. Barb is bored. Eggsmerelda and Eggbert are bored. Actually, we're only bored

until Phil comes over. He makes Barb and me laugh. . . . Yesterday he brought over some books and read them to all of us. *Make Way for Ducklings* is a personal favorite.

5. Sorry I didn't thank you right away for the receiving blankets. The twins looked wonderful in them. . . .

6. I didn't do anything on Halloween except give out candy. Little Bo dressed up as a can of worms.

I'm sorry that you couldn't get through to IM me. I had to block incoming messages so I could concentrate on doing research for a paper for Mr. Izzard.

I'm also sorry that I don't feel like talking much now. I'm very tired.

Love,
TSTARR

P.S. I'm not sure that I'm going to go to the play.

Date: November 7 8:23:48 PM
From: Eliz812
Subj: And Once Again . . . Dad
To: TSTARR

Dear Tara★,

Are you going by TSTARR now instead of Tara★?
(That's how you've been signing some of your e's.)

I have a lot to tell you, but before I get started, a few
questions: How is Barb? How are the twins? Did you
really dress Little Bo as a can of worms? If you did,
what did his costume look like?

The big news around here is that Dad showed up
again. Yesterday (Saturday) Mom and Emma and I
were sitting in the living room with Howie and Mr.
Besser, who had dropped by on their way to run er-
rands so Howie could return a library book for me.

The doorbell rang and there was Dad. Emma hadn't seen him since he left last spring, and she was all shy and apprehensive around him. Then she noticed the bag of Gummy Worms he was holding and she became friendlier. Dad announced that he was there to take Emma to the movies. At this, I saw Mom and Mr. Besser glance at each other. The reason was obvious. Dad was drunk as usual.

"Did you drive here?" Mr. Besser asked him.

Dad seemed to notice Mr. Besser for the first time. "Who's he?" he asked Mom.

Mom introduced them.

Dad just nodded. Then he held out his hand to Emma.

"Wait a second," said Mom. "We haven't discussed this. Emma can't go with you."

"I have a right to see her. She's my daughter," said Dad.

(Tara, I ask you — not that I really care, but aren't* I his daughter too? How come he's so focused on

*I know "aren't" isn't correct here, but "am I not" sounds SO old-fashioned.

Emma? Maybe it's because she's little and not already mad at him.)

Anyway, Mom said, "You should have called first. Besides —"

"Besides, you've been drinking," interrupted Mr. Besser.

Needless to say, that did not go over well with Dad. He tried to deny it, but then he stumbled over absolutely nothing.

"I think I'll call the police," said Mr. Besser, "and tell them you're driving while intoxicated."

Dad looked all smug at that and said, "I came by bus."

Well, that was interesting. Maybe he doesn't have a car. Maybe he came over by bus the last time too. Who knows?

I'd been looking back and forth between Dad and Mr. Besser. Now I looked at Mom again. She was absolutely furious. "I told you never to come here drunk again," she said quietly. "And yes, Emma is your daughter, and I suppose you do have a right to see her, but I will not let you take her away from this apartment when you've been drinking. Now, please leave."

"You can't keep my children from me," said Dad.

"Maybe we'd better decide that in court," Mom replied.

Dad backed off then. I thought he was just going to walk out the door, but instead he turned to Mr. Besser and said, "You stay away from my wife." <u>Then</u> he left.

Tara, I wanted to <u>disappear</u>. Can you imagine how embarrassed I was?

The second Dad had left, Mom and Mr. Besser went into the kitchen and I could hear them talking quietly. I couldn't even look at Howie. But before I had a chance to burst into tears, or to make a run for the bedroom, Howie swung Emma up in his arms and said, "Who wants to go get ice cream?"

"Me!" cried Emma.

So we waited about ten minutes in case Dad was hanging around, and then we went out, leaving Mom and Mr. Besser behind. The walk to Dair-E Freez completely distracted Emma from Dad's visit. And it distracted me a little bit. Enough to see that Howie doesn't think I'm some kind of alien, even if my father is.

I have decided that Howie is one of the greatest people on this planet.

I'll keep you posted.

Love,
Elizabeth

Date: November 11 8:45:22 PM
From: TSTARR
Subj: And Once again . . .
TO: Eliz812

Dear Elizabeth,

Hi . . . I'm back to Tara★. I tried out TSTARR for a while but don't like being called that. (It's fine for my e-mail address, though.) You know me. I like to try out new things. My hair this week, by the way, is a lovely shade of puce. . . . Just kidding.

Anyway . . . wow . . . your father came back. He is LOWER than pond scum, to show up drunk to take Emma out. And he's so mean to exclude you. (Not that you would want to go with him, but still that's soooo hurtful.)

Wow. . . . Your mom was incredibly strong. She has changed sooooo much! And Mr. Besser really got involved. That's so amazing. I wonder if he and your mom are getting "involved" too. I am so glad he and Howie are in your lives, whatever way it is.

What about Emma? I can't believe ice cream so easily distracted her from what was a really powerful scene. Maybe when she's older and in therapy or something, it will all come back to her and she'll deal with it then.

Elizabeth, I can't believe that in the middle of telling something so big, you would take the time to worry about word choice. That is sooooo YOU.

Now for what's happening in the Lane House (and outside environs):

1. Little Bo Poop has lost his pinworms . . . and can't tell where to find them. For Halloween, I made a tube to go around his body, drew on it so it looked like a soup can, and labeled it Campbell's Cream of Worms Soup. He was not happy wearing his costume.

2. The twins are fine. The project is almost over. Some kids say that when we are done, they are going to hold a "Smash Them" day and break the eggs and then have a party. Phil and I have de-

cided we will come back to my house, blow out the liquid from each egg, and then each keep one of them. (I'll probably take Eggsmerelda. Phil does not have a strong fashion sense.) Or maybe we will share custody. I really do think Phil is terrific and I am soooo glad we are friends. Actually, he is getting cuter and cuter the longer I know him.

3. Bart came over yesterday to apologize and ask if we could get back together. He was so sweet. He brought candy for me . . . and flowers for Barb. (I think his older brother coached him.) We talked for a while and I told him I didn't want to go out with him again, that he had acted like a jerk. (He agreed that he had acted like a jerk.) We talked for a while more and decided to be friends. (I am learning so much this year, it's amazing.) So he isn't perfect, but he's still worth knowing. After our big talk, he and Barb and I played Scrabble. It was nice.

4. About Luke . . . He is just the best dad. (I hope you don't mind my saying that.) He is going to school, working, and doing his best to help out around the house. The other day I walked into

my parents' bedroom and Luke was resting his head on Barb's stomach and singing "Hello Baby" (to the tune of "Hello Dolly") to the baby. Barb was kind of patting him on his head. I almost turned around to leave them alone but they told me to come in and join them. We all sat there singing songs to the baby. I sang "Sisters." (Luke says that if the baby is a boy that might confuse him.) It was one of the best times in my life. It was so "family." I really do love my parents soooooo much (even though they drive me nuts sometimes). And I'm prepared to give the baby a chance. I'm not promising to adore her but I'm beginning to think of her as part of the family, of *my* family.

5. About Barb . . . I saved this part for last because there's so much to say and at the same time, not so much. She's doing OK. There was a scare the other night. She thought she was going into labor again but she wasn't. (She's giving up pizza with sausage until after the baby is born.) She's not great at staying in bed, but she's managing . . . reading a lot of books and watching too much television. Sometimes I feel

like I'm her personal servant, but most of the time I feel like we are "mother-daughter bonding," which is something they talk about on those daytime TV shows. (I confess. I've been watching them with her.)

6. It's hard to come right home from school when all my friends are staying to work on the play and the yearbook, and for just having fun. But my friends have been terrific, coming over here . . . calling . . . talking on e-mail . . . and Instant Messaging.

Phew, this is a very, very long e-mail. You can tell I am spending a lot of time at home.

Elizabeth . . . do you think we could work out a time and day when we could IM each other? It would be so great if we could do that. I'm going a little stir-crazy . . . and I do miss "conversing" with you.

Lots of Love,
Tara★

Date: November 13 2:13:13 PM
From: Eliz812
Subj: Thanksgiving
To: TSTARR

Dear Tara★,

Well. Of all the developments. You won't believe what happened this morning. (Don't worry. It isn't Dad related. And it's a good thing.) The phone rang, Mom answered it, talked for a few minutes, and then came into the living room, where Emma and I were watching *Charlotte's Web* on TV (I just love rainy Saturdays). She said Mr. Besser had called and wanted to know if we would like to join him and Howie for Thanksgiving. It's going to be the first Thanksgiving they've actually celebrated since Howie's mother died. (She died not long before Thanksgiving last year, and Howie said he and his dad were too sad to celebrate either Thanksgiving or Christmas then.) And of course, this will be our first Thanksgiving since Dad moved out. So . . . we're going to do it. We're going to have the meal at Howie's because his apartment is bigger than ours, but we're going to share the cooking equally. I can't wait. This is going to be so much fun! It won't be a BIG Thanksgiving celebration like we're used to, but I just know it's going to be better.

One worry — what if Dad calls and wants to know what we're doing for Thanksgiving? Maybe he'll expect us to spend it together. I know Mom won't change our plans, but still, how will we handle this? Maybe this is something I should leave in the adults' hands. I guess so. I don't know. I have a funny feeling about Dad and the Bessers and Thanksgiving. (But mostly I'm really excited.)

You know, I've been thinking about Howie, Tara. There have been those times when I've felt certain strong sensations when I'm near him — like the heat from his hand in the movies that time, or just . . . I don't know, weird, powerful vibrations when we're alone together. But I'm still not sure I feel anything more than a really wonderful, close friendship with him. You know how it is (how very exciting) when you first discover that a person is more of a soulmate than just a regular friend? You must have felt that at some point with Hannah, and maybe with Phil too. And I remember the first time I felt that with you, even though we were pretty young then. It was the fourth or fifth day we'd eaten lunch together in the cafeteria, and suddenly we discovered that we both like to write, that we both keep journals, that we <u>adored</u> *Harriet the Spy* because it's a journal. Remember that? I bet you do. At the time I just thought you were my new best friend. But looking back I see that what I was feeling was the discovery of a soulmate. I kind of think that's what I feel with Howie, except that I've never felt that way about a boy before, so maybe I confused what those feelings meant. Oh, Tara, I hope you understand what I'm saying. I don't know if I'm making myself clear.

All right. On to a different subject.

I love what is happening with you and Luke and Barb right now. You are so lucky. Nothing has REALLY changed in your family, and yet you're all growing so close. (And no, Tara, of course I don't mind if you say what a great dad Luke is. I like hearing about great dads. Maybe that's one reason I like Mr. Besser.

Knowing about people like him and Luke gives me hope, even if I've given up hope with my own dad.)

Gosh, that's scary — what happened with Barb and the pizza. But you know what, Tara? I just have a good feeling about the baby. I really do. I think she's going to be okay.

Oh — I just reread your e, and yes, I'd LOVE to set up a time to send IMs. What about tomorrow afternoon? Any time is fine with me. Three o'clock might be good, because Mom is taking Emma to a birthday party then. Let's leave it at 3:00, unless I hear from you. (I promise to check my e-mail tonight and tomorrow morning.)

Enjoy the rest of your Saturday, Tara!

Love,

Elizabeth

P.S. A question for those kids who are planning "Smash Them" day. Have they thought about what those eggs might smell like by now?

Date: November 13 11:58:53 PM
From: TSTARR
Subj: It's been a great day . . . and night!
To: Eliz812

Hi, Elizabeth,
Luke took the day off and stayed home with Barb. . . .
And I went out and had a GREAT time. I went to the
high school football game. Our team lost but I won.

Why, you ask?

I found out that Phil is an outstanding kisser. (We
started out kissing every time our team scored but
then we decided to kiss when either team scored!)

I think you should stop worrying about how you feel
about Howie and just enjoy it. It sounds like the two of
you are turning into really close friends and that's very
special.

I guess the main thing I understand about relationships between boys and girls is that I don't understand them . . . but since we've just started our teenage years, I'm not too worried. We have a lot of time to figure everything out.

As for Thanksgiving, yours sounds wonderful with the Bessers. If your father wants to come, tell him you'll already have one turkey at the table and that's enough.

After the game, we all went to a party at Jada Murphy's house. . . . Lots of dancing.

I am soooooooooooooooooooooo tired.

Talk with you tomorrow.

I can't wait.

Love,
Tara★

November 14 3:03:46 PM

INSTANT MESSAGE

Eliz812: Hi. It's me!

TSTARR: Elizabeth . . . I am sooooooo excited. . . . I'm soooooooo glad we are "talking." . . . There is so much to tell you . . . so much to hear!

Eliz812: I know! I can't believe we're actually talking! How are you? How is Barb?

TSTARR: She's OK . . . getting a little stir-crazy. Remember the pot holders we used to make? Well, she's taken my old loom out of "storage" and is making pot holders. Pitiful, huh?

Eliz812: What's she going to do with them?

TSTARR: She said either she's going to make a baby quilt or she's going to throw them out. She can't decide. For a while she threatened to make a vest for Luke out of them but he said he wouldn't wear it.

Eliz812: Ha!

Tara, I'm dying to know — did the kids in your class really hold "Smash Them" day?

TSTARR: They did . . . although a few kids picketed as Right to Lifers and said the eggs shouldn't be "killed." I think a little reality testing needs to be done on some people. Phil and I have saved our eggs as souvenirs, but we did go to the party. . . . It was an eggscellent party, by the way.

Eliz812: Very funny!

Okay, before we really start talking, I have to know how long we can IM. (You know I like to know these things ahead of time.) I think I shouldn't stay on more than about 15 mins. because I shouldn't tie up the line for too long.

TSTARR: OK. Fifteen minutes. I wish we could stay on for hours, but I have to be careful too. Luke may try to call and check in on Barb. (She's doing well, but we all still worry a lot. . . . There have been a few problems.)

Eliz812: What kind of problems? How worried should I be?

TSTARR: Don't worry. It won't do any good. That's what my parents say to me (although I can tell that they are a little worried too). There has been a problem with something called "spotting" and every once in a while Barb thinks she is going into labor, but the longer she stays in bed and the baby isn't born the better it will be. So don't worry. I think everything will be OK.

Eliz812: Well, like I said before, I have one of my strong feelings about this baby — that SHE is going to be fine. (Are you thinking about names yet?)

TSTARR: We're starting to. The other day Luke (Beatles lover that he is) suggested Penny, as in Penny Lane. I like the name Tamara. Barb is still thinking about it.

Eliz812: How about just plain Mary? That's one of my favorite names. (Emma suggested Barbie.)

TSTARR:Aaaaaaaarg . . . Barbie . . . aaaaaaaaaaaaarg. And while Mary is a perfectly fine name, it just doesn't have enough flair. What is happening at your house? Is a romance heating up between your mom and Mr.

Besser? You and Howie? Emma and anyone? And what is happening with Emma's school?*?????????

Eliz812: Hmphhhh. No flair. Thanks a lot.

Well . . . Emma's school. No news so far, except that Mom is still talking with the parents of a bunch of kids here at DEER RUN who are all in the same boat.

Howie and me — what I told you the other day. I think he is turning into one of my very best friends. It's just that it's so strange for a best friend (of mine) to be a boy.

TSTARR: Don't be offended. I guess the name Mary has "flair" but Tamara, Lucinda . . . those names make me think of someone who will lead a dramatic life . . . not that someone named Mary can't.

What about the teachers at the school? Won't they need jobs??? Is there a room at DEER RUN that could be turned into a day-care place?

I am not going to get bent out of shape because Howie is now your best friend. I know that I am still one of your best friends and I don't want to waste time discussing it again. I know there are different kinds of best friends for different reasons . . . and I just want to say how glad I am that we are still able to talk to each other about important things.

Eliz812: Definitely. Me too. But I didn't say Howie was now my best friend. I said, as I've said before, that he's ONE OF my best friends. Anyway, what I meant about Howie is that our feelings for each other (as far as I can tell) are not boyfriend/girlfriend, but best friend/soulmate . . . which is so new for me.

Emma's day care: There are 4 teachers. 2 have found jobs at other day-care centers (the fancy ones we can't afford), 1 is moving (was going to move anyway), and I don't know about the 4th. But one thing Mom is looking into is a day-care center in the home of one of Emma's friends here whose mom has her child-care license, or whatever it's called. She MIGHT quit her temp job and start a day care for the four DEER RUN kids.

TSTARR: That would be wonderful.

Uh-oh . . . Barb has just called out that she is making a diaper cover out of the pot holders. . . .

Eliz812: I bet Emma would wear a vest made of pot holders if we told her Barb made it for her. It's a little mean, but it would give Barb something to do.

TSTARR: It will make Barb soooooooooooooooooooooo happy. . . . Are you sure Emma won't mind? She really is a terrific kid.

If my baby sister turns out to be like Emma (with more jewelry), I would be soooooo happy, although I do think I will be a bossier big sister than you are.

Eliz812: Emma is truly great. And you should see her when she plays dress-up. Maybe you had more influence over her than you realized.

Oh — I never answered your question about Mom and Mr. Besser. You know, I think something is going on there. Not sure how serious it is (Howie and I love it, though!) or how long it will last, but . . . it's exciting.

TSTARR: Do you think that with all the things that are going on, our lives are turning into soap operas or just real everyday lives with easy and hard stuff mixed in???? If they are soap operas, I wonder what the commercials would be like?? We could advertise pot scrubbers . . . or pot holders.

Eliz812: Or my father could do a beer commercial!!!

Tara, I hate to say this, but we have been on for way longer than 15 mins. Mom is probably going to bring Emma home from the party soon. I think we better get off. Okay? Give my love to Barb and Luke. And XX to you too.

TSTARR: Aaaaaaaaaaaaaaaaaaaarg . . . I was having such a good time. My fingers are turning into "chatterboxes." OK, I know we have to stop now. . . . Love to you, your mom, and Emma. Looking forward to your next e-mail.

Eliz812: Bye! I'll write soon!!

TSTARR: Bye.

Date: November 17 5:10:45 PM
From: Eliz812
Subj: Just a Note
To: TSTARR

Dear Tara★,

I almost sent you an e-mail the moment we ended our IM chat on Sunday, but I didn't really have anything to say except . . . that was so much fun! It was nearly as good as being on the phone.

Not a whole lot has happened in the last three days. Mom and Emma's friend's mom, Mrs. Randall, and the other moms are still talking about having a small day-care center in the Randalls' apartment.

Howie and Susie and I are working hard on *Silhouette.* The first edition is almost finished. Remember last spring when Mrs. Jackson said we would put out three editions this year and I wrote to you that I was SURE we could do four? Well — Mrs. Jackson was right!! There's no way we can put out four editions. It is SO much work. I think we'll get the second one out at the beginning of March and the third out when school ends. And that will be cutting it close. Mrs. Jackson was doing a lot more work on *Silhouette* last year, work my staff and I do now, so everything takes longer. Plus, most of the kids have sports and plays and dances and other after-school activities in addition to homework and *Silhouette.* Anyway . . . I'm working on a poem about glistening icicles.

No word from Dad, which is good, of course. Maybe we'll get away with a peaceful Thanksgiving. Luckily, Dad doesn't know about our plans or where the Bessers live.

How is Barb doing?

Another possible baby name—Marianna. I thought of that while Susie and I were walking to school today. (Howie got up late so his father drove him.) I like Marianna because it's pretty fancy, but it still has Mary in it. What do you think?

Tonight I am going to fix spaghetti for supper. I'm getting pretty good at cooking, Tara. Then Mom and Emma and I will have a nice, cozy, quiet evening. On most weeknight evenings we all play a board game (Emma's choice — usually Candy Land) after dinner. Then Mom and Emma read together and have bathtime for Emma while I do my homework. After Emma goes to bed, Mom and I talk and have hot chocolate (Emma doesn't know about the hot chocolate!) and finally Mom and I go to bed too. I just love our evenings. They are so different from the ones we used to have in our old house, especially the ones after Dad lost his job, when Dad would drink and he and Mom would talk and fight and try to figure out what they should do, and I would try to finish my homework and take care of Emma, keep her out of earshot of the fighting. Even going to bed wasn't very nice. I could still hear the fighting. Now we go to bed and I hear . . . Emma breathing. Period.

I just love our new peaceful life.

Okay . . . spaghetti water is boiling. Gotta go.

Love,
Elizabeth

Date: November 20 11:08:39 PM
From: TSTARR
Subj: The Play's the Thing
To: Eliz812

Dear Elizabeth,

I loved our IM chat too!!!!! It's such a shame that our computers are on our family phone lines so we can't chat endlessly. (I hope someday I can get my own computer and put it on my own phone line. . . . Someday . . . rats . . . *someday*. . . . I want it all now, even though I know I shouldn't. As Barb says, "Tara★, Patience is not your middle name.")

Speaking of names, there is still no decision on the baby's name. Luke says we should wait to see the baby before we decide, but I think we are all a little nervous about whether the baby is going to be OK. (We are in "the safety zone," though. . . . The due date for the baby is Dec. 12, and that's only three weeks away. THREE WEEKS . . . wow!!!!!)

About the play . . . Tonight I went to it . . . met Phil there and Hannah and the rest of the gang. I had lots of feelings about it.

1. I was soooooooooo glad to get out of the house and do things with people. (Although during intermission I did phone home to make sure Barb and the baby were all right. They told me to stop worrying and enjoy myself. . . . So I did, sort of.)

2. What I didn't enjoy was seeing stupid Lisa in MY part. . . . I just know I would have been a lot better. (She even forgot some lines at one time. I know she did. I know that part by heart.) I especially hated the curtain call when people applauded her and she got bouquets of flowers. (She had a lot of relatives in the audience.) I know I'm being crabby about this but I can't help it.

3. Bart was in the audience with his new girl-friend, Marti Bloomfield. She's really nice. I wish her luck!

So there you have it . . . my night at the play. I had a great time with my friends, but this tiny part of me (OK . . . no so tiny) wanted to be up there being a STAR . . . Tara★, the Star . . . and wanted people to applaud me, and wanted to get the flowers, and go to the cast party.

You know something, Elizabeth . . . now that I'm home and thinking about it, I wish I could have had it all . . . the play, the time at home with Barb, everything. But I didn't . . . and that's OK too.

Anyway, that's it for now. (I am very tired.) Please e-mail soon. I want to hear all about you . . . and your family. (Any further developments with your mom's romance?)

I hope your father leaves you alone on Thanksgiving. That would make everyone thankful.

Love,
Tara★

Date: November 25 3:42:21 AM
From: TSTARR
Subj: IT'S A GIRL
To: Eliz812

It's a girl. . . . SHE'S A GIRL. . . !

I wish I could call you right now and talk to you, but it's the middle of the night. I can't wait to talk with you tomorrow, though. (I will call you after I go to the hospital to see the baby, and I'll give you a full report. I don't care how much of my allowance it costs, I just have to talk with you "in person" and anyway, there will be special rates on THANKSGIVING Day!!!!!!!)

The baby has a name. . . . No, it's not Mary, sorry. . . .

She was born with red hair. (Luke says it's sort of his color but really, really red.) So her name is . . . TA-DA . . . A DRUM ROLL HERE . . . her name is Scarlett.

(It figures she would be named after the main charac-
ter in Barb's favorite book, *Gone with the Wind*. After
all, I was named after the plantation in that book. If I'd
been born with hair that red, I'd probably have been
named Scarlett. . . . Weird to think about that.)

Luke says she is perfect. She was only a little early, just
about on time. And she's healthy, fine, and he says "absolutely beautiful." (I will not be jealous. . . . I will not
be jealous. . . . I will not be jealous.)

Tomorrow, I will decide for myself. More details to fol-
low then.

Love,

Tara★ (Now a big sister too. It's nice to have something else in common with you when our lives are
changing so much.)

P.S. HAPPY THANKSGIVING

Date: November 25 8:19:57 AM
From: Eliz812
Subj: SCARLETT LANE!!
To: TSTARR

Dear Tara★,

I don't usually check my e-mail first thing in the morning, but since today is a holiday . . . I did. And I am so glad I did!

I can't believe she is here! And she is fine! (See? My strong feelings are usually right.) And she is a girl! YESSS!! (We were both right about that.)

I really like her name. It's not Mary, but it's a good name. You and your sister have theme names. . . . Hmm. If Scarlett grows up to be anything like the Scarlett in the book, you better watch out. She is going to have a mind of her own. (And you better not

208

let her near draperies if she says anything about a new dress.)

I have to go. Mom needs me to help with the cooking this morning, but I'll talk to you later today. We're going over to the Bessers' around 1:00 and we'll probably be there all afternoon. Maybe you should call in the evening. If I don't hear from you by 8:00, I'll call you, okay?

I can't wait to talk to you!!!!

Tell Barb and Luke CONGRATULATIONS!!!!

Lots of Love,
Aunt Elizabeth

Date: November 25 5:58:07 PM
From: Eliz812
Subj: Thanksgiving at the Bessers'
To: TSTARR

Dear Tara★,

We just got back from the Bessers' and there was no message on the answering machine from you so I checked my e-mail. I see that you're going to call me in an hour. I barely know what to do with myself for the next hour because I'm so excited about Scarlett and because we had such a nice Thanksgiving, so I thought I'd kill the time by e-ing you about our day. (I figure we'll only talk about Scarlett this evening.)

Tara, we had the BEST time. For starters, Dad didn't call. I was so afraid he would; that somehow he would manage to spoil the day. But he never called. We cooked peacefully, with the Macy's Thanksgiving Day Parade on TV in the background. Mom and Emma and I were responsible for the turkey (Mr. Besser said he has as much knowledge about turkey cooking as he does about atomic energy) and rolls and dessert. Mr. Besser and Howie took care of salad, vegetables, condiments, and hot spiced cider.

A little before 1:00, Mom and Emma and I set out for the Bessers'. Because of the turkey we had to drive there, even though their apartment is only a few buildings away. Emma thought this was hysterical.

Anyway, the afternoon was SO NICE, Tara. It was really relaxed. And it was SO DIFFERENT from the huge Thanksgivings we used to have with Dad's family. (Remember the awful one last year? When he'd lost his job but hadn't told anyone yet, and we really couldn't afford the gala day he'd planned, but he insisted on having the dinner anyway? Horrible.) But not this year's. First we sat around the Bessers' living room and talked and drank cider. (Howie has a two-bedroom apartment with a dining room. It seems huge!) Then we moved into the dining room for the meal. Mom sat at one end of the table and Mr. Besser at the other. Howie and I sat next to each other (across from Emma) and we kept nudging each other under the table — whenever we saw Mom and Mr. Besser exchange a look or something. I'm not QUITE sure what's going on with them, Tara, but they seem awfully familiar with each other.

After the main part of the meal we took a break, and Howie and Emma and I played board games while Mom and Mr. Besser cleaned up the kitchen. Howie and I started to help them but they shooed us away. Very subtle.

Later we ate dessert. Before we were served the pie, Mr. Besser handed out party poppers. Some old Besser family tradition. So we ate the pie with these silly paper hats on our heads.

Sigh.

I think it was a perfect afternoon.

And now I am waiting for your call; waiting for news about Scarlett.

Talk to you in a few minutes!

Love,
Elizabeth

Date: November 26 3:26:08 PM
From: TSTARR
Subj: The Report
To: Eliz812

Dear Elizabeth,
As promised, here is the report.

I know that when I talked with you I spoke very quickly . . . and it was hard to keep track of everything.

It's just that I was sooooooo excited.

Barb is fine. . . . Now that I know she is fine, I can tell you that I was very worried something terrible would happen and she would die and it would be my job to raise the baby. (I know there was no reason to believe that, but I kind of did. . . . Phil says sometimes

I can be a real drama queen, but I was very worried about losing Barb and about being left with a baby. Phew.)

You asked me to write down the vital statistics.

Scarlett Lane:

She weighed 6 pounds, 1 ounce at birth.
She is 19 inches long.
Her hair is soooooooooooo red.
She looks fine . . . for a baby.
The only jewelry she has on is her hospital bracelet.

She's OK, my sister. . . . I have no idea what she's going to be like later, but she's OK.

To be honest, I'm not totally excited about Scarlett, the sister, the person. I'm just glad she and Barb are in good shape.

Time will tell how much I am involved with her.

Is it selfish that I am soooooo glad that now I can go to school activities again?

Even though I missed being in *Annie,* I'm going to try out for the next play.

Oh, before I forget, I want to say that I have a lot to be thankful for this Thanksgiving. . . . For Scarlett, for the fact that you were so happy this holiday.

I've got to go.

Barb, Luke, and Scarlett will be coming home . . . HOME . . . any minute.

Love,
Tara★

P.S. I feel a little weird.

Date: December 6 4:57:31 PM
From: Eliz812
Subj: Christmas and More
To: TSTARR

Dear Tara★,

I'm sorry I haven't written in so long. I really didn't mean for more than a week to go by. But I've been very busy (as I'm SURE you have). And I have, at least, been thinking about you every day. Did Scarlett get the package I sent? Did you get the card I sent? Can you believe you can buy cards that say "Congratulations, big sister!?" What do you think of the outfit I made Scarlett? I know it isn't as fancy an outfit as you would make, and I know it won't fit her right away (maybe in a few months) — but, well, anyway, it comes to her with lots of love.

I'm not surprised that you feel weird, Tara. You've been an only child for so long, and suddenly you have to share your parents and your room and your life with a baby. I know you've known about the baby for a long time, but it's impossible to predict how an event (any event) will actually feel. We have to experience it first. It's like when my family decided to move last spring. We started packing, we had the auction to sell our stuff, Mom showed Emma and me the apartment at DEER RUN, and so forth. But after we'd moved, I did feel weird for a long time, even though I also felt better.

And, Tara, don't worry about how much time you feel like spending with Scarlett. Remember — she's Barb and Luke's baby, not yours. Five years from now you'll be away at college. I mean, I think it would be wonderful if you bonded with the baby and just adored her and everything, but don't give yourself a hard time if you're ambivalent about her. She's your sister, not your child. And of course you should be getting involved with things at school again. (Mom always tells me that school is my "job.")

So . . . now that Scarlett is home, how <u>does</u> it feel? How is everything going? Is she sleeping in your room at night, or in Barb and Luke's? Are there any baby-related things that you particularly like doing? What do Barb and Luke let you do (besides dress her)?

Well . . . I'm afraid I have more Dad news. Every time I get my hopes up and think he's out of our lives forever — he shows up again. I was <u>so</u> relieved and thankful when he didn't call about Thanksgiving. I thought maybe that meant he had moved away or something. (Actually, what I hoped was that because he had seen Mom and Mr. Besser together he would think we were getting on with our lives and he wouldn't try to be part of them anymore. But that was wishful thinking.) Dad called last weekend and told Mom he wants to spend Christmas with us. He said Christmas is a family time. Can you believe that, Tara? What a joke. Well, to be perfectly honest, I know that we are a family, but still, to hear him say that after everything he's done . . . Mom's reaction was pretty much the same as mine. She told him we have plans for Christmas (if we do, I don't know any-thing about them), but he argued with her for a long time, and finally she gave in and told him he could come over on the day after Christmas if he wanted. She also told him that Howie and Mr. Besser would be here then. Now — I would think I'd know about day-after-Christmas plans with the Bessers. I could tell Mom just made that up on the spur of the moment. And you know what, Tara? I don't think she made it up to try to keep Dad from coming. I think she made it up because she's afraid to be alone with him — I mean, not to have another adult around. I was already feeling a little afraid of Dad, but now, just knowing that Mom is afraid too, I suddenly feel <u>more</u> afraid.

Anyway, the rest of the story is that Dad agreed to stop by the day after Christmas, even knowing Mr. Besser would be here, and Mom has since arranged for Howie and Mr. Besser to actually come over that day. (How embarrassing.)

I'll keep you posted.

Love you lots!
— Elizabeth

Date: December 11 10:02:55 AM
From: TSTARR
Subj: Babies — Your Father, My Sister
To: Eliz812

Dear Elizabeth,
Don't feel bad that you haven't e-mailed in a while. I understand. . . . I've been really busy too.

I do wish your father would just go away forever. There's no reason for him to be bothering your mom and you and Emma. Maybe you'll get lucky and he just won't show up on the day after Christmas. You know . . . he promises to do something and then he doesn't. Hopefully, he'll repeat that pattern. Or maybe you'll get lucky and he'll have drunk so much alcohol that when he lights a cigarette he'll just explode. (I hope you don't mind my saying that . . . and anyway, I don't think it could really happen. Sometimes when I say bad things about your father, I feel guilty even though I keep thinking about how your father deserted everyone on the day you were all supposed to move to the apartment. He really doesn't deserve the consideration your mom is giving him.) Anyway, it is very smart of your mom to have Mr. Besser and Howie at your house when he comes. I just hope your father doesn't make some dumb humiliating scene. Although if he does, you should try not to be too embarrassed. It's not your fault he's so awful.

I just hope he doesn't show up.

About everything you have sent . . . that outfit with the smocking on it is so beautiful. I know you've been working on it since last summer, but still . . . how do you manage to make those things? And the cute little buttons . . . Elizabeth, you are a real artist!!!!! We are all in awe. Luke said we are just going to have to find some special place to go to so Scarlett can dress up. Then we realized that the rest of us don't own clothes that wonderful, so Scarlett will wear the outfit to celebrate her first Christmas. We'll take a picture of her in it and send it to you. As for the cards, it was great that you found the perfect one for each of us. You are sooooooo thoughtful.

Barb requested that I ask you if the potholder vest for Emma arrived yet. She says she is sorry some of the loops are not sewn down. She wants you to know she's so busy that she no longer had time to work on it, so she sent it out before it was quite finished. (Elizabeth, between us . . . I would totally understand if Emma pukes when she sees it.)

As for me and the baby . . . thanks for all the advice. In some ways, the baby's birth has been wonderful for me. I have more time for myself. My parents aren't watching what I do as closely as they were before.

I think the baby's OK. . . . I don't have any heartwarming bonding stories to tell, nor do I have horror stories. I'm hoping that Scarlett's first word will be "sequins." Actually, I think I'm adjusting better to Scarlett than Little Bo is, now that he's no longer the baby in this family.

The next play will be *You're a Good Man, Charlie Brown*. I'm going to try out for the part of Lucy. Luke says if I get it, it will be typecasting, but I THINK he's teasing. I'm not that bossy!!!!!!!!!!!!!

Some of my friends and I are on our way to the mall to do some Christmas shopping. Ho-ho-ho. . . .

Much Love,
Tara★

Date: December 18 2:25:19 PM
From: Eliz812
Subj: Christmas and SNOW!!
To: TSTARR

Dear Tara★,

It is exactly one week before Christmas and it is SNOWING!!!!! I am so excited! I don't care whether we get enough snow to close school. I just want the snow to last until Christmas Day. I'm looking out the sliding door here in the living room, and the courtyard is a fairyland. The snow has been falling since early this morning. We probably have six or seven inches so far. I already had to take Emma outside to make a snowman. It's standing at the edge of the patio — carrot nose, a scarf, a hat, and marble eyes.

Oh, Tara, I am also soooooooo excited about Christmas. I know it's going to be really different from last year. It'll be the first Christmas in the apartment, and Mom doesn't have much extra money, so there won't be a lot of gifts, but I'm <u>still</u> excited. Howie and Susie and I will exchange presents (we made plans for Christmas Eve Day), and I'm excited about a lot of the presents I've made for people. Plus, we're going to have Howie and his dad over for Christmas dinner. <u>Plus</u>, Nana and Grandpa are thinking about visiting us sometime during the week between Christmas and New Year. (They'll have to stay in a hotel, though, because there isn't room for them in our apartment. They're a little too old to sleep on the floor. And their only other choices would be the convertible sofa in the living room without any privacy, or the bunk beds in Emma's and my room. I don't think so.)

Anyway.

Tara, I don't mind the things you said about my father. You know I don't like him any more than you do. The only thing I disagree with is your saying there's no reason for him to be "bothering" Mom and Emma and me. Unfortunately, he has a right to do this. Not to bother us but to remain in our lives. He IS still Emma's and my father, and he and Mom aren't divorced yet. So legally I think he has a right to see us. I wish he didn't, but I don't make the laws. I don't think Mom can bar him from the house; not without putting our custody in jeopardy, and believe me, she does NOT want Dad to wind up with even partial custody of us. So she's following the rules now.

About whether Dad will actually show up on the day after Christmas — I don't know and I don't care.

On to more pleasant topics. Yes, the potholder vest arrived. Don't tell Barb, but I kind of laughed when I saw it. I mean, she did a really nice job on the individual pot holders, but when they're all sewn together . . . well, they just make an odd-looking vest. I hope you don't mind, but I haven't given it to Emma yet. Since it's going to be a slim Christmas, I thought I'd save it for the big day. I wrapped it in Santa paper and put a tag on it that says TO EMMA FROM BARB. It'll be one more gift for Emma under the tree.

Tara, thank you so much for what you said about Scarlett's outfit. That means a lot to me. Are you really going to take a picture of her in it on Christmas? I can't wait to see it!! (I do think the outfit is going to be a bit big on her then, though.)

On Monday I'm going to mail a box to you and Barb and Luke and Scarlett. It should get there before Christmas. Don't you love all the surprises and secrets that go with Christmas?

I think of you every day, Tara. Scarlett too. I try to imagine what she's doing. Do you have any idea how old babies are when they begin to smile?

When are the auditions for *You're a Good Man, Charlie Brown?* I REALLY, REALLY, REALLY hope you get the part of Lucy. You deserve it.

Deck the halls and all that.

Love,
Elizabeth

Date: December 21 6:34:51 PM
From: TSTARR
Subj: Christmas is almost here!!!!!!
To: Eliz812

It's a winter wonderland here in Ohio. In fact, we've had two snow days in a row. I bet you think I am overjoyed about the snow days, but I'm not. As weird as it may seem, I'd rather be in school.

Do you have any idea how loudly our little bundle of Scarlett can cry???? That baby has a very healthy set of lungs. Right now she is sleeping in my parents' bedroom (her parents' too . . . I know), but one of these days, I am going to have to share my room with her. (I will never be able to call it "our" room.)

It's kind of weird. I worry about her a lot. When we did the egg project, we learned about SIDS . . . Sudden Infant Death Syndrome . . . and now I get very nervous wondering whether she's all right. I go check on her a lot when I am at home. . . .

One day when Barb was napping I watched Scarlett. I literally just sat there and watched her. Oh, and I had a discussion with her (OK . . . a lecture . . . it would be a discussion if she could talk back, and she can't do that yet). I talked to her about fashion and style . . . about being an individual . . . about being creative . . . about how she should always do whatever her big sister says.

About your dad . . . I'm nervous. What if he actually does show up? Do you think he will be drunk? Do you think he will say or do something to Mr. Besser? Do you think he will try to get back with your mother? Do you think maybe he is going to AA meetings and getting better? Do you think he will let you tell him how you feel about what happened? Will he listen? What if he does something weird or crazy? These are some of the things I think about.

What are you planning to do with your grandparents? How do you think they will feel about Mr. Besser and Howie? Will your grandmother make her spiced apple cake, and if so, would you please send me a piece?

My Christmas is going to be fun. I'm going caroling with the gang, and then there is going to be a party on Christmas Eve Eve (that's right — the day before Christmas Eve). Then on Christmas Eve my family will trim the tree, and then it's Christmas. On the day after Christmas, Hannah's family is having a party for all of their friends. (Yes, Phil and his family will be there. Luke is being very embarrassing and referring to Phil's parents as the "in-laws.")

Your package arrived today. I think it is wonderful that Emma decorated the brown wrapping paper with Christmas decorations. I especially liked Rudolph the Purple-Nosed Reindeer. I can't wait to open the presents.

I hope my package arrived at your house, and that your family loves the presents. . . . I wish I could be there to see your face when you open yours.

Anyway, joy to the world. Happy holidays!

Love,
Tara ★

Date: December 25 8:35:12 PM
From: Eliz812
Subj: CHRISTMAS!!
To: TSTARR

Dear Tara★,

I can't believe it. Christmas is (basically) over. Every year it seems to take forever to come, and then — suddenly — it's over. Well, it isn't really over. We'll celebrate again when Nana and Grandpa come, plus, there are still about 3½ hours left this evening, but . . . you know what I mean.

Tara, we had the nicest day, although it started on the early side. Emma found it impossible to stay in bed beyond 5:30 AM, so we all got up then. This year there was no grand staircase to run down in order to see what Santa brought, and our tree is puny compared to the mile-high ones we used to get. On the other hand, there was no drunken dad sitting around in his bathrobe all day, handing out gifts he couldn't afford to buy. Anyway, Emma and I hurried into the living room and woke up Mom. Right away, we had an interesting dilemma. Emma asked Mom point-blank if she had seen Santa (since Mom sleeps in the living room), and how he had arrived (since we have no fireplace). You want to hear Mom's answer to those questions? She put her hand to her mouth and cried, "Oh, my gosh, Emma! Look what's under the tree!" When Emma saw her very own roller skates (thank you, Value Town), she nearly had a heart attack. And she completely forgot about her questions (or else she's starting not to believe in Santa and didn't want to press the issue in case we said something she didn't really want to hear). Anyway, the next hour was a blur of looking through our stockings and opening presents. We finished opening everything before 6:30. That's SIX-THIRTY AM. Oh, well. We just had a nice quiet morning after that. The afternoon was spent getting ready to have Howie and Mr. Besser over for dinner. I could just go on and on about the rest of the day and about our presents, Tara, but I better not. Before I answer all the questions you asked in your last e, though, let me just say two things:

1. Mom and Emma and I LOVED the presents you sent. Did Barb help you pick out the perfume for my mother? Mom said it was perfect, and that it's been a long time since anyone has given her perfume. Emma spent nearly half an hour putting those stick-on glitter stars on her fingernails. Oh, and she really liked the pot-holder vest. She wore it to dinner, in fact. (I think this is one of the great things about being five. You just love all your presents, no matter what they are.) And Tara, the necklace is wonderful. Truly. You made it, didn't you? I bet you got the supplies at that sewing and crafts store you took me to. Anyway, I do love it. I'm wearing it now.

2. We had a truly great dinner — all relaxed and cozy. And Howie gave me this book about women poets. I gave him cuff links that look like computers (not sure he'll wear them). In fact, we all gave each other presents, but I was most curious to see what Mom and Mr. Besser gave each other. She gave him a

sweater, he gave her earrings. (What, if anything, do you think these presents mean?)

Okay, on to your questions: I just have absolutely no idea about what might happen tomorrow if Dad arrives. Will he actually show up? I don't know. There have been those memorable times when he didn't show up. And those memorable times when he showed up unannounced. We know he'd like to buy back Emma's affection with presents, so here's a good opportunity. Plus, he said something to Mom about having a big surprise for us. I think <u>Mom</u> thinks he's going to show; otherwise, she wouldn't have bothered to ask Mr. Besser to be on hand. As for all of your other questions except two, I can only say once again, "I don't know." The two questions I think I can answer are, "Do you think he will let you tell him how you feel about what happened?" and "Will he listen?" And my answer to both is no.

My grandparents — 1. We're just going to do regular (inexpensive) family things — make popcorn and watch videos, go to Chuck E. Cheese, maybe go to the skating rink. And we'll have a Christmas celebration the night they arrive. 2. I think they will like Howie and Mr. Besser very much. 3. Yes, I think

Grandma will make the apple cake — but I don't know how well it will fare in the mail!

Oh, Tara, I hope you had a wonderful Christmas, your first with Scarlett. I understand about watching over her the way you do — and about not particularly liking her healthy set of lungs. Everyone could live without the sleepless nights that babies bring. But then . . . there's so much more to babies. You'll find that out as Scarlett gets older.

Merry Christmas, Tara! And if we don't e in the next few days, Happy New Year too!

Love,
Elizabeth

Date: December 27 1:25:28 AM
From: TSTARR
Subj: News . . . news . . . news . . . please . . .
To: Eliz812

Dear Elizabeth,

It's the day after Christmas . . . actually a little past the day after Christmas . . . and your father was supposed to come to your house and you haven't let me know what happened!!!!! It's making me crazy. Barb said to respect your privacy . . . that this is a really major deal in your life, and that you will tell me in "your own good time." (Barb keeps reminding me how different we are and that I can't expect you to do things the way I do. But still, THIS is so major.) Anyway, I want to know not just because I am curious, but because I am really concerned. I don't want to think about what could have happened if your father came into the house drunk, angry, jealous. . . . I'm trying not to be tooooooooo dramatic about all of this, but if I knew what happened, my imagination wouldn't run wild. So please let me know what is happening.

It is very late . . . or very early . . . to be writing this e-mail, but Scarlett Lane has made her presence known once more. She is just the loudest crier. I think maybe she was awakened when Luke was yelling at me for coming in sooooooooo late from the party at Hannah's. I guess he didn't appreciate my calling him from Hannah's for a ride home after he and Barb had gone to bed. But I can't help it if Scarlett has been keeping them awake at night, and if he has to get up sooooooooo early to go to the college library to study.

Barb seems to be a little depressed lately. She says that happens sometimes after giving birth. She said she was very depressed for a while after she had me. (Let me tell you . . . that's something I really liked hearing . . . that my birth depressed my mother. But by the time I was old enough to understand things, she was fine, so I expect she will pull out of it for Scarlett too.)

Life is very different at the Lane house. One of the good changes is that the computer is out of the living room, so I can use it in my room.

Elizabeth, I have a question. (I know . . . I have a lot of questions.) This is an e-mail one. How can you NOT check your e-mail every day?????? I check mine all the time . . . at least twice a day. (Also, some of my friends and I send Instant Messages a lot.) And if I'm not careful, there are a gazillion messages piled up in my mailbox, awaiting my answer. Doesn't that happen to you? When you haven't checked your e-mail, don't you wonder what's in it???? Sometimes I think you miss the old days, when we sent letters to each other. Is that true? I'm just curious about all of this.

About Christmas . . . We had a great time. (Once we get them developed, I will send you the pictures we took. You will see how beauteous Scarlett looks in the outfit you made. And you will see how we all look now. I think you will agree that Luke looks quite handsome with his new beard . . . and that my red hair looks quite festive with the green streak in it.) Friends stopped by and we sent out for pizza for our meal. (I realize that my family doesn't always do things like a lot of the world, but pizza seemed right . . . and the delivery guy showed up in a Santa suit, so that was fun.)

Presents . . . I got clothes and jewelry . . . not a lot . . . but I really liked what I got. Scarlett "gave" me cute earrings. I got her books, including a wonderful POETRY book (I know you'll appreciate that). It's called *You Read to Me, I'll Read to You*. (When Scarlett is old enough, she'll be able to read the easier poems. Until then I will read both parts, using two different voices.) Also, I got her some George and Martha books.

As for your presents, they are just sooooooooooooo wonderful. When do you find time to make such beautiful things? The beaded barrette is splendiferous, and your latest collection of your own poetry is really amazing. (I just wish some of it wasn't so sad!) Little Bo is just wild about the catnip mouse you sewed for him. Luke loved his notebook. You decorated it so well. When did you learn to decoupage? Barb loves the place mats. We used them with our Christmas dinner and were very careful not to get pizza sauce on them.

Speaking of presents . . . Howie's cuff links. Does Howie own any shirts that need cuff links? I don't know one single boy who owns a shirt that needs cuff links, but maybe Howie's different. Just curious. I'm sure the ones you got him were wonderful.

Anyway, I'm getting tired, so I'm going to sign off.

Please let me know what's going on at your house, and I hope I hear from you before New Year's, but if not, have a happy one.

Much Love,
Tara★

Date: December 28 7:57:07 PM
From: Eliz812
Subj: my stupid father
To: TSTARR

Dear Tara★,

Sorry I didn't write you right away. Dad's "visit" was
a nonevent, so I didn't feel as if I had anything much
to tell you. What happened on the day after Christmas? Absolutely nothing. Because Dad didn't show
up. Again. Wasn't that what I said might happen? I
don't know why I got all geared up for a visit, what
with his history of <u>not</u> showing up. Maybe it was because he said he had a surprise for us. Or maybe it
was because Mom made such a big deal out of making sure Mr. Besser would be here when Dad arrived.
MOM certainly thought he was going to show up.
So . . . he wasn't drunk, angry, or jealous. He didn't

have inappropriate presents for Emma. He didn't have a showdown with Mr. Besser. Nothing.

Howie and Mr. Besser came over at about two in the afternoon (an hour before Dad was supposed to arrive). They were still sitting here at six-thirty, so we sent out for Chinese food, ate it, and when Dad STILL hadn't arrived, they finally went home. And that is the end of that story.

I don't know what to think. Once again, I am relieved. I was so afraid of an embarrassing encounter between Dad and Mr. Besser — with Howie watching. Or of something worse. But I'm also disappointed. I don't know why I want to feel that someone so hideous as my father cares about me, but I do. So now I am hurt. <u>And</u> relieved. Which is a very strange combination.

About my e-mail . . . I don't know why I don't check it more often. I guess mostly because while I like getting e-mail, there are things I like better than sitting in front of the computer and answering it — such as reading, sewing, or seeing people in person. E-mail is fun, but there's nothing like actually spending time with people. To be honest, sometimes my e-mail (not the letters from you, of course) begins to feel a little like homework. And my homework is something I try to get out of the way so I can do fun things. Yes, plenty of letters pile up in my mailbox, but I figure I can answer them just as easily by spending one hunk of time at the computer every couple of days as I can by sitting down at it several times a day. Plus, I think you are right, Tara — I do kind of like snail mail better than e-mail. It's just more . . . personal, I guess. Especially if it's handwritten, but even when it's typed or written on the computer. How often do you save a piece of e-mail? Almost never, I bet, even if you print it out. How often do you save snail mail? Well, I don't know about you, but I save most of it. I have every single piece of snail mail you've written to me since you moved.

Nana and Grandpa arrive this evening. In fact, Mom and Emma are at the airport picking them up right now. (I said I wanted to stay behind and be by myself for a while.)

Howie's cuff links — What do I know about boys? Or cuff links? To be honest, I'd never seen Howie wear cuff links, but I thought maybe boys wore those cuff link shirts on special occasions like bar mitzvahs or

Christmas dinner. In any case, Howie seems to like them, so that's a good thing.

I'm sorry I'm so crabby, Tara. I'm not mad at you, you know. Maybe Nana and Grandpa will improve my mood.

More soon.

Love,
Elizabeth

Date: December 29 8:56:44 AM
From: TSTARR
Subj: Can't Be Reached
To: Eliz812, PhilRup, Palindrome, Sarabeth111, NotA-Goofup, KateiK, nanlew, marcm, kittycat, booger, teenortot, inafog, susieq, sarahheartburn, Eddieiz, futureactress, blob, cookielover, kidinnj, cyberteen, pizzahog, tunaburger, petra, littlemo, lillipop, jimjohn, wiseguy, frenchfry, Alarmclock, bartboy, skibum, cdrob, cindella

I'm grounded until Jan. 1. . . . Can't use phone . . . no e-mail coming or going . . . twenty-five words or less to say this. . . . Happy New Year.

Aaaaaaaaaaaaaaaaaaaaaaaaaaaaaaaaaaaaaaaaaaaaaaaaarg.

Date: December 29 2:20:51 PM
From: Eliz812
Subj: WHAT DID YOU DO?
To: TSTARR

Dear Tara★,

I know you won't be able to read this for three more days, but WHAT HAPPENED? Even I couldn't NOT respond immediately to an e like the one you sent. (Also, I'm thinking that just <u>maybe</u> you'll find some way to sneak into your e-mail before New Year's Day. If you do, PLEASE WRITE, even if it's just another 25-word note.)

I can't imagine what happened. Whatever it was, was it really your fault? Does it have to do with Scarlett?

With Phil? Some kind of over-the-holiday homework assignment?

I'm dying to know.

Love,
Elizabeth

Date: January 1 7:12:01 AM
From: Eliz812
Subj: HAPPY NEW YEAR — NOW PLEASE WRITE TO ME
To: TSTARR

Dear Tara★,

Okay, it's New Year's Day. Your grounding should be over. So please write to me ASAP and tell me what happened. As you can see from the time at which I'm writing this, I am beside myself wondering. (Well, I suppose you can also see that I didn't really stay up all that late last night.)

All right. Let me fill you in on the last few days.

It's been great having Nana and Grandpa here. I'm in a much better mood. We celebrated Christmas again, which was SO nice. We did the whole thing — presents under the tree and another dinner (this time Nana and Grandpa cooked). And we've done pretty much everything else I told you we might do. Also, Nana and Grandpa took us out for a really nice dinner two evenings ago. We got all dressed up and went to Blue Mountain. Yum.

Last night . . . New Year's Eve . . . Howie and Susie and I all went to a party at Maura Hansonmeyer's. (She lives at DEER RUN too. Her family moved here at the beginning of the school year.) The party was really fun. But if you can believe it, not one single guest had permission to stay out past 10:00. So I watched the ball drop at home on our television with Mom, Emma, Nana, Grandpa, Howie, and Mr. Besser. At the stroke of midnight, we opened out sliding door and we could hear people cheering and yelling, and even a couple of firecrackers going off. Then Mom poured champagne for the adults, and sparkling cider for Howie and Emma and me. It was nice (but I was in bed by 1:00).

Okay, Tara, get this — Mom has started divorce proceedings. I'm not quite sure how all of this works, but I know that she and Nana and Grandpa have seen Mom's lawyer a couple of times. I think maybe Dad's not showing up on Sunday was what finally made

Mom take charge of this. (Well, that and Mr. Besser. I'm pretty sure she wants to be serious about him, but she can't be until things are straightened out with Dad.)

Okay, I've about exhausted my supply of things to tell you.

Please write, please write, please write.

What happened?

Love,
Elizabeth

Date: January 1 9:01:12 AM
From: TSTARR
Subj: I'm Ungrounded!!!!!!!!!!!!!!!!!!!!!!!!
To: Eliz812

Dear Elizabeth,
You are the very first person I am writing to, now that my "sentence" is over. I wish I could call you.

Barb and Luke were really really really angry with me. I haven't been able to go out at all since THE PARTY . . . at Cindi's . . . Dec. 28th. . . . It started out OK, but then a couple of kids snuck in some liquor and beer in knapsacks . . . and some of us drank it. I had two cans of beer, one taste of Southern Comfort, two sips of Bailey's Irish Cream, and a mouthful of scotch. I thought the beer had a disgusting taste, but when you mix everything together it's totally revolting, especially after onion dip, potato chips, and green olives.

And then I really felt sick . . . and rushed to the bathroom. (I know you are hating all of this, Elizabeth, and I don't blame you! It was soooooooooooooo dumb.) But there was a line for the bathroom. (There was already a kid in the bathroom being sick.) Someone in the front of the line started barfing, and that got me started, and two other kids also . . . and then it was a total group barf. (I did think of Karen Frank and how she always barfs on the first day of school. Well, this was much worse!)

Cindi's parents (who had spent the night in the kitchen with friends having a party of their own) came out to investigate. They were very mad (and not just because of their new wall-to-wall carpeting). The party was canceled and we all had to call our parents to pick us up.

Luke picked up Hannah and me. Hannah and I both threw up in the backseat. Luke was very angry, and I said something I shouldn't have . . . that he never got angry when Scarlett spit up.

After we dropped off Hannah (her parents were angry too), we went home.

I went into the bathroom and threw up some more. I don't know when I've ever felt that sick.

Then I went into the living room, where my parents were waiting. I got a major lecture.

Elizabeth, I told them I was sorry. I really was . . . and am . . . sorry. I don't understand why anyone in his or her right mind would want to get drunk. It was disgusting and no fun . . . no fun at all. I felt dizzy and sick and like I was being a dumb, bad person.

It wasn't enough just to tell my parents I wouldn't do it again. They made me sign a pledge. . . . I am not allowed to smoke, drink, or do drugs. (I wasn't planning on smoking or doing drugs. You know how disgusting I think those things are.) So I promised. I signed the paper.

Then they told me I couldn't go out until New Year's Day . . . no New Year's Eve party for me . . . and I wasn't allowed to communicate with the outside world until now.

Elizabeth, don't you be angry with me too. I know I was being dumb, not thinking . . . but now I know what it's like to drink, and I know I won't do it again. So the experience wasn't a total loss. Since your father is an alcoholic, I know you must have really strong feelings about what I did. But I'm just a kid . . . and no one is perfect.

Anyway, I spent a lot of time with Scarlett. She was the one person in the house who didn't look angry and sad when she saw me . . . and she didn't lecture me every three minutes.

I told her never to drink alcohol.

Anyway, now you know.

Love from your sorry friend,
Tara★

Date: January 1 10:46:46 AM
From: Eliz812
Subj: (no subject)
To: TSTARR

Tara —

I am trying SO HARD not to be angry, but I can't help how I feel.

What a stupid, stupid thing to do. Of course I have strong feelings about it.

I know you said NOT to be angry with you, but please . . . you're a <u>kid</u>? No one is <u>perfect</u>? What kind of stupid excuses are those?

I don't really want to talk with you right now, Tara. And don't bother writing to me. I can't answer you for a while.

— Elizabeth

Date: January 12 4:37:10 PM
From: Eliz812
Subj: I hope we're still friends
To: TSTARR

Dear Tara★,

I don't know how long you can hold on to e-mail
you've sent, but my last letter to you is still in my
computer. I just read it and I feel awful. I still think
that what you did was really dumb (and maybe dan-
gerous), but I know that I shouldn't have gotten angry at you. And that the reason I did get angry
doesn't have much to do with you. You were right
when you said that because of my father I must have
strong feelings about drinking. I have REALLY strong
feelings about it. I don't want you (or anyone) to become what my father has become. I don't ever want
to see you wobbling around, slurring your words,
ruining your life — and hurting practically everyone
you know. What you did at the party wasn't anything

like that . . . like my father. But Dad had to start somewhere, didn't he? Was it at a party when he was thirteen? Maybe he didn't like the taste of liquor then either. Or maybe he did. I don't know. Anyway, I was thinking more about Dad than about you when I wrote you that note.

What I'm trying to say, Tara, is that of course I don't want you to become like Dad, but I also heard what you were saying in your letter. I know you had a terrible experience, and that you meant it when you said you won't drink again. I know too that you were serious when you signed the pledge.

Do you think we can be friends again, Tara? I'll understand if you say no. We've talked about how our friendship is already changing. We are two <u>very</u> different people. And my last note was really harsh. Maybe we can't (won't ever) be as close as we were when we lived in the same town, went to the same school. And as you said once, maybe we wouldn't have stayed close even if you hadn't moved. But I hope I haven't ruined things completely. I would miss you very much if you weren't in my life in <u>some</u> way.

Love,
Elizabeth

Date: January 20 9:10:52 PM
From: TSTARR
Subj: Friends?
To: Eliz812

I'm glad you can see that you were soooooo angry at me because of your father. I hate, though, that you've never been able to let him know how angry you are at him . . . and that I got so much of that anger.

After your first e-mail I was mad and very hurt. I *did not* want to be your friend anymore, not ever again. I don't think you have the right to dictate when I can talk with you or when I can "bother writing to you." When you get angry, you just back off until you get calm again. I don't think that's a bad thing all the time, but it is a definite way for you to be in control, to be a . dictator . . . not to allow the other person to react, to say what she feels. It's not always so neat and tidy, even if you want it to be that way.

So are we going to be friends again, Elizabeth? I never stopped being *your* friend.

We are so different. I think we are not only different, but we are always going to have differences . . . and that's OK with me. What's not OK with me is when your answer to dealing with something is to push me away. Since I got your letter last week, I have done some very serious thinking, and no, I don't want to be pushed away like that. You know, Elizabeth, it's a little like when we were younger and used to illustrate our writing with pictures. You always liked coloring in the lines and I didn't. I think that's the way we are about a lot of things. But that doesn't mean that one picture is better than the other, that one is more "perfect." They are just different.

I don't think we can ever be the kind of friends we used to be . . . but it's true, we wouldn't have been the same kind of friends if we still lived near each other.

What I think is that as we grow and change our friend-ship grows and changes. (Whew . . . this is a lot more serious than I usually am, but this is very important to me.) I hope we always like and respect each other, and understand that neither of us is perfect. (Over the last few weeks, I think we have shown that neither of us has been "perfect.")

I guess we'll just have to wait and see what happens to our friendship and find out if it lasts.

— Tara★

Date: January 21, 4:09:39 PM
From: Eliz812
Subj: Friends? continued
To: TSTARR

Dear Tara★,

Thank you for writing back. I'm a little confused, though. I think you still want to be friends, and you talked a lot about our differences and our continuing friendship, and said, "I never stopped being your friend." You also said that after you got my first e-mail you did not want to be my friend anymore, not ever again, and that we'll just have to wait and see what happens to our friendship and find out if it lasts. So . . . I guess now we're waiting and seeing?

You know, Tara, I have been trying for months to let my father know how angry I am at him. If I haven't told him, it isn't for lack of trying. You think I make myself unavailable to you sometimes? Try confronting someone who's moved out of your life, who doesn't have a phone or an address (that I know of), who doesn't show up when he says he's going to. Remember last spring when I prepared that list of questions I was going to ask him? When I was all ready to sit down with him and make him give me answers and tell him what I thought about a few things — and then he came to our apartment when he knew no one would be home? I understand that this doesn't excuse my directing my anger at you, but I hope you realize that if I haven't let him know it's because it's kind of like trying to tell something to a dead person. That's how available he is. When I was angry at you these last few weeks, you, at least, could have written to me, even if you thought I wouldn't respond. But I don't even know how to get in touch with my father.

Although, wait — something just occurred to me. If Mom and Nana and Grandpa have been meeting with a lawyer about divorce proceedings, then Mom must know how to get in touch with Dad, right? So maybe I can talk to him soon. I mean, get in touch with him myself and do something on my own — not wait for him to say he's going to come over and then not show up.

Anyway, Tara, I do want to continue our friendship (I never stopped being your friend either). I meant it when I said I would miss you very much if you weren't in my life in some way. And I guess we both agree that we are awfully different, and that our friendship is going through some changes and probably would have done so even if you were still living in New Jersey.

With all that agreed on — where do we go from here? Can we start by just catching each other up on our news? I miss doing that. I haven't told you what happened with Emma's day care, or what's going on with *Silhouette.* Or about Howie and the cuff links. (I'll tell you really quickly, just in case this isn't okay with you yet.)

Day care — Katie Randall's mom did start a day-care center in her apartment here. So at lunchtime, Mom picks Emma up at kindergarten and drives her to Katie's apartment. And now I pick Emma up at Katie's whenever I feel like it in the afternoons. If I want time to myself, or if I have a *Silhouette* meeting or whatever, I can leave her there. If I want to bring her home, I can do that too. The nice thing about this arrangement is that Mom gets home a bit earlier now and everyone is a little less frazzled in the evenings.

Silhouette — the first issue came out and was a big hit. We're hard at work on the second issue. I'm composing a poem about violets called "Nature's Swans."

The cuff links — Howie's birthday was last week and guess what his father gave him. A shirt that he can wear the cuff links with. Mom decided to splurge and take all of us out to dinner at T.G.I. Friday's, and Howie wore the shirt and the cuff links. He was the most dressed-up person in the whole place. (He looked wonderful.)

That's the news. I hope you write back soon, Tara. I really do.

— Elizabeth

Date: January 21 9:29:51 PM
From: TSTARR
Subj: I Can't Think of One
To: Eliz812

Dear Elizabeth,
Of course I'll write back soon! I always do. Well, almost always.

Let's not worry so much about our friendship, okay? Let's just have it.

Soooooooo . . . I don't have a lot of time right now. I still have homework to finish. Plus, I have 49 more lines (49 out of 200) to write of I WILL NOT TALK IN DETENTION. (I got detention for talking in class.) Scarlett is still not talking, although I've tried very hard to teach her the word "accessorize."

Guess what. Our school has a big-deal Valentine's Day dance each year AND . . . Phil just asked me to it. You know, Elizabeth, this is the first time a boyfriend of mine has been a friend first. I think I like that. What do you think?

Gotta go.

Love,
Tara★

Date: January 22 4:01:48 PM
From: Eliz812
Subj: Hearts . . . Candy . . . PHIL
To: TSTARR

Dear Tara★,

A Valentine's Day dance. That is so romantic. And Phil asked you to it. I am <u>so</u> excited for you. You are going, aren't you, Tara? Do kids get dressed up for this big-deal dance? Can you wear a red dress?

I think it is GREAT that Phil has been a regular friend first and now is a boyfriend.

Something just occurred to me. Do the girls buy the boys boutonnieres to wear to this dance? You could get Phil a red carnation. You

Mom just came home from work early — said I have to get off the computer now — has to talk to me. Very upset. More later.

Love, E

Date: January 22 9:12:01 PM
From: TSTARR
Subj: Horrible horrible news
To: Eliz812

Dear Elizabeth,
It's so hard to believe.

I don't know what to say.

I love you.

I'm sorry that something so bad happened.

I just can't believe your father is dead.

I knew something was wrong when you didn't send another e-mail after you talked with your mom. I started to worry. Then I just got this awful terrible feeling. . . . And then your mom's phone call came. Barb told me everything after she got off the phone.

Elizabeth, such terrible news.

Dead. . . . Your dad, driving drunk. . . . Thank goodness no one else was hurt. I am so upset about you and your mom and Emma. I guess there *are* more people who were hurt in the accident — the three of you.

Love,
Tara★

P.S. I will understand if you don't e-mail me for a while.

Date: January 23 5:48:32 AM
From: TSTARR
Subj: How are you doing?
To: Eliz812

Dear Elizabeth,

I haven't slept all night thinking about what happened and worrying about you and your family.

I woke Barb and Luke up at 3:00 AM and we talked for a long time.

I'm so upset.

As you've said, even though you had all those problems with your father, he was still your father. . . . I keep thinking about what the police officer told your mom — that your dad probably died instantly when the car hit the tree. As awful as that is, I'm so glad he didn't have to live through the explosion. I hope knowing that makes you feel a little better in this awful time.

I know you don't check your e-mail every day even when things are good, but if you are checking it, please know I'm thinking of you. And I hope you let me know what is happening.

Much much much love,
Tara★

Date: January 23 11:02:53 PM
From: TSTARR
Subj: Please let me know how you are!
To: Eliz812

Dear Elizabeth,

I know it's probably a little selfish of me to ask you to think of letting me know how you are doing when things are soooooooooo hard for you . . . but please . . . let me know.

I'm worried — you've said before you wished your father were dead. I hope you don't feel guilty about saying that, or that you feel you caused his death. Wishing something doesn't make it happen.

I'm also worried because I know how hard it is for you to show your feelings (even though you've gotten much better at it in the last year) . . . and I worry that it's all going to stay inside you and make you sick . . . or that you are going to be hysterical and out-of-control crying. (I know I would be if something ever happened to Barb or Luke. It's just so awful.)

Barb says you are going to go through lots of feelings over time and that it's part of the "process." She also said to tell you we are all available to talk if you want to.

I wish I could call you this very instant and hear your voice and know how you are doing right now . . . how your mom is . . . how Emma is handling all of this. But I know I have to wait. (Barb and Luke said I have to wait, to let you and your family handle this in your own way.) So even though it is very hard, I'll wait.

I love you lots,
Tara★

P.S. Please give Emma a special hug for me.

Date: January 24 4:39:12 PM
From: TSTARR
Subj: Another e-mail from me
To: Eliz812

It's me . . . Tara★ . . . just checking in to let you know I'm thinking about you. How are . . . Listen, I know I should wait . . . but I can't. I'm sending this e-mail to show you I'm trying to wait . . . but it isn't working.

I'm going to call your house right now.

Love,
Tara★

Date: January 24 5:29:18 PM
From: TSTARR
Subj: The phone call
To: Eliz812

Dear Elizabeth,
Well, no one was there . . . but I did get to leave the message asking you to check your e-mail if you can. I hope I did an all right thing. I just care so much. . . .

Love,
Tara★

Date January 24 7:24:56 PM
From: Eliz812
Subj: (No subject)
To: TSTARR

Dear Tara★,

Got your message. I'm so confused. I hardly know what day it is. Or what time. This is the first I've been alone in the apartment since the accident. Nana and Grandpa just arrived. Mom took Emma over to their motel. I said I didn't want to go.

Tara, Mom is a mess. I'm so worried about her. She can't stop crying. Part of me doesn't understand. Dad hadn't acted like my father or her husband for months. Hadn't lived with us for months. So why are we so upset? Mom just cries and cries and cries. I've never seen anything like it. I cry all the time too. And there's no privacy here because people are always coming by. They bring stuff, mostly food. None of us wants to eat, though.

Emma looks like she's in shock. I don't know what she's feeling. She won't talk to me. Anyway, I have a lot to think about.

Love,
Elizabeth

Date: January 24 8:03:44 PM
From: TSTARR
Subj: Thanks for the e-mail
To: Eliz812

I'm so glad you e-mailed!!!

I know you have a *lot* to think about.

Just know that I'm here to listen.

Much Love,
Tara★

Date: January 24 10:31:38 PM
From: Eliz812
Subj: (No subject)
To: TSTARR

Dear Tara★,

I'm back.

You know what I've done for the last two days? Nothing. I've hidden in my room. I don't want to see people. I don't know what to say to anyone.

Nana and Grandpa finally left a while ago. I'm glad. Emma and I went to bed. I couldn't sleep. Got up. Heard sounds coming from the living room. Went out to see what was happening. Tara, you wouldn't believe it. I didn't. Mom was sitting on the sofabed, crying. She had started to make the bed and had stopped before she had even pulled it out all the way.

She was just sitting on the edge of it, crying so hard. Her shoulders were shaking. She was gasping. I didn't know what to do. Now she's in the bathroom crying. It's scary. Mom <u>has</u> to be in charge. If she isn't, then who is? What if something happens to Mom? What would happen to Emma and me?

How am I going to get through the next few days? Howie and Susie and everyone keep stopping by, but I don't want to see them. I don't want to see anybody. But if you were here, I would want to see you.

The funeral (well, really the memorial service) is on Saturday. I don't want to go. I don't want to be alone. I don't want to be with people. I don't know what I want.

I don't know how often I can write to you, Tara. People are always here, and the computer is in the living room, so I can hardly ever use it privately.

Love,
Elizabeth

Date: January 25 8:31:27 PM
From:TSTARR
Subj: We'll Be There
To: Eliz812

I'll be there to go to the service with you . . . to stay with you at the apartment . . . whatever you want. If you want to talk, we'll talk. If you don't want to talk, we won't talk.

Luke and I will be flying in on Friday morning and leaving on Sunday afternoon. Barb and Scarlett will stay in Ohio because Scarlett's got a little cold and can't fly . . . and three plane tickets are a lot.

We'll be staying at the Blakes' house . . . and I can spend as much time with you as you want.

I just want for you not to feel so bad.

Love,
Tara★

Date: January 25 9:49:49 AM
From: Eliz812
Subj: (No subject)
To: TSTARR

Dear Tara★,

It's early and no one has come over yet. Mom and Emma just left to pick up Nana and Grandpa to bring them back here. They're going to finalize "arrange-ments" today.

I can't believe you're going to be here.

Thank you.

Can you come right over here on Friday? I want to see you as soon as possible.

Love,
Elizabeth

Date: January 31 9:02:38 PM
From: TSTARR
Subj: Checking In
To: Eliz812

Dear Elizabeth,
Now that I'm back home in Ohio, I just keep thinking about everything and want to check in. I don't know what to say except that I feel so bad for you. I just want to let you know that.

Love,
Tara★

P.S. Luke and Barb send their love too. And Luke says you're very brave.

Date: February 1 5:21:39 PM
From: Eliz812
Subj: Back to My "Life"
To: TSTARR

Dear Tara★,

I still can't believe you were here. I can't believe the
funeral was three days ago. I can't believe Dad's
accident was more than a week ago. I can't believe
he's dead.

I was SO glad you were here. I know I said that thou-
sands of times, but it's true. I don't know how I
would have gotten through last weekend without
you. I guess there's just nothing like a best friend. I
mean, an original best friend. As soon as I saw
you . . . well, you know what my reaction was. I
thought I had already cried all the tears I had. I
guess not.

And the funeral. What a nightmare. Have you ever seen anyone cry like Mom was crying?

And Emma — thank you for taking her out of the chapel to calm down.

It was so weird to sit there and listen to all those people talk about my father, remembering the person he used to be, instead of the person he had become. Tara, I feel really bad saying this, but you know what the VERY WORST thing about all of this is? Now I'll never know why Dad did any of the things he did. What happened to him? What went so very, very wrong? Why did he start drinking? Why did he leave us? Why did he do all those stupid things, like buy Emma a stereo when he had absolutely no money? Why did he try to stay in touch with Emma and not with me? I don't understand any of it, and now I never will. This stupid accident is the most horrible of all the horrible things he's done to us.

I have more to say, but Emma's yelling about something. Again.

More later.

Love,
Elizabeth

Date: February 1 5:52:49 PM
From: Eliz812
Subj: Back to My "Life" (cont.)
To: TSTARR

Dear Tara★,

I'm back. It's quiet now. But Emma is having such a bad time. She's confused about everything, so she doesn't like to let Mom or me out of her sight. She made a real scene yesterday morning and this morning when it was time for Mom to take her to day care. Screamed and yelled and threw herself on the floor. For some reason, I have no patience for that. This morning I told her to shut up. But then I felt bad and told her I'd pick her up early this afternoon. Which I did. She's here now, watching *Mulan* and sucking her thumb.

I went back to school today. Back to my "life." But it feels unreal.

Love,
Elizabeth

P.S. I am trying so, so hard to write a poem about Dad, but I can't.

Date: February 1 9:25:29 PM
From: TSTARR
Subj: Life in Ohio Gets Back to Abnormal
To: Eliz812

So much to talk about. . . .

The funeral . . . Yes, it was a nightmare. There's so much that was weird. I didn't think your mom could cry like that. She never seemed very emotional to me. . . . Barb says there are some people who just keep it all inside. That's what I thought your mom was like. So it was kind of scary to see her get hysterical. . . . And your dad's ex-boss, the guy who fired him, talking about what a good worker he was. (If he was such a good worker, why was he fired? Oh, I know it was a business decision and that a lot of people were fired, but the boss just seemed so phony.)

I hope your mom didn't get mad at us for laughing during the funeral. . . . It was very funny, though, that the minister is allergic to flowers and has to do funeral services surrounded by them. The best part, of course, was when he sneezed into his hand and didn't know what to do with the gunk.

And now that it's over, I can fill you in on some of the stuff you don't know about. . . . Karen Frank barfed in the sink of the ladies room at the chapel . . . and I overheard a couple of the girls from your homeroom talking about who was the best dressed at the service . . . saying that "black is such a grown-up color to wear." I guess I'm telling you some of this to try to make things seem not sooooo heavy, so rough. But it really is sooooo heavy, so rough. . . .

About Emma . . . I feel bad for her. She's too young to have all this bad stuff happen to her. . . . But then so are you.

Oh, one more thing. . . . I think Howie is a great friend for you. I especially liked when he told off that stupid guy who used to work with your dad. I know the guy didn't see us, but he had no right to say your dad was "just an accident waiting to happen." It's obvious Howie cares about you, that he listens and tries to do what's best for you.

Knowing he and Susie are in your life made it a little easier for me to go home.

You asked me to keep you filled in on what's going on here. I hope the following report helps take your mind off of things — for a few minutes, anyway.

Scarlett is almost over her cold. . . . Her sneezes aren't so goopy anymore. (Sometimes she gets it on *our* hands!)

Barb is going stir-crazy . . . wants to go back to work early . . . has made arrangements for Scarlett to go back with her.

Luke has been trying to spend a little more time with me. I think he got freaked out by your dad's funeral. (He says any time you need a "dad type" to talk to, he'll be available.)

As for writing a poem about your dad, maybe you shouldn't try to force it. When you are ready, it will happen. Until then, maybe you could write a poem about something else.

I'm so glad we got to spend some time together, even for such an awful thing.

Love,
Tara★

Date: February 5 1:53:17 PM
From: Eliz812
Subj: Poems
To: TSTARR

Dear Tara★,

I've been thinking about what you said about writing
a poem — that I should write one about something
other than Dad or death. So I tried to write one about
life and birth. This is what I came up with:

Summer Mountains

Pointing to the sky,
Capped with clean, white snow,
Hearing fir trees sigh,
As gentle winds do blow,
Are the mountains grand,
Beauties of the earth,

> Rising from the land,
> Since this planet's birth.

Now that I've finished it, I think it's stupid. I still can't come up with a poem about Dad. I feel like my poetry is leaving me.

I got a D on a social studies assignment. I just didn't feel like working on it. Mom was mad.

Mom is getting a little better, I think. She cries less. Last evening Mr. Besser took her to dinner.

Yesterday was the first morning Emma didn't throw a tantrum when Mom said it was time to go to Katie's. I suppose that's progress.

I liked hearing your news, Tara. Tell me about the Valentine's Day dance. I know that's coming up. Are you excited about going with Phil? Have you decided what you are going to wear? Is Hannah going to go?

I know Howie is good for me. He is a good friend too. I think I've been crabby lately, and Howie just keeps coming over anyway. So does Susie. And they find me all day long at school — walk with me between classes, sit with me in the cafeteria, in the library. I'm not sure I've told them how much it means to me. Especially when a lot of other kids don't know what to say, and I feel like they're all looking at me.

I better go. Mom wants to spend this afternoon writing notes to all the people who sent us things or came by after Dad died. She wants me to help her. She said we have over 200 notes to write.

Love,
Elizabeth

Date: February 9 7:59:22 PM
From: TSTARR
Subj: It's a bird! It's a plane! It's superskier!!!!!!!!!!!!!
To: Eliz812

Sorry it has taken sooooooooooooo long to write back, but I've been away. Hannah and her family took me SKIING. . . . That's right. SKIING. (Wow . . . do you notice that the two capitalized I's in "skiing" look like skis? . . . Amazing!!!!!!!!!) Anyway, we went last Friday night and were supposed to come back on Sunday, and then there was a BLIZZARD. (Do you notice that the two Zs look like a skier who doesn't know how to go in a straight line? Well, that was me, Tara★ Lane!) We had to stay two extra days. It really was fun. Next time I may even graduate from the "baby" slopes. . . . And next time, I'm going to decorate my ski mask with rhinestones and sequins!

About your poem, I think it is NOT stupid. Having just been on winter mountains, I can definitely appreciate your ode to summer mountains.

I'm glad your mom isn't crying so much and is trying to get back to "normal." It must be so hard for her. . . . I guess she must have still loved your dad or something. I'm glad she and Mr. Besser went out the other night.

I hope Emma is acting better. Poor kid.

About your D on the social studies assignment . . . no one's perfect. It happens sometimes. . . . At least it does to me.

As for the Valentine's Day dance, I'm still going with Phil. He has a T-shirt with a "tuxedo" stenciled on the front and back. He'll wear that with a pair of black trousers and Nikes.

I will wear a short black skirt, combat boots that have been painted with glitter, and a pink fuzzy-looking sweater.

Yes, Elizabeth . . . I am excited about going to the dance with Phil. I am excited about so many things. I like being a teenager.

Is there going to be a Valentine's dance at your school? If so, I really think you should ask Howie. Let me know what's happening.

I hope your hand doesn't fall off from having to write all those letters. If you were planning on sending one to my family, you don't have to. . . . That will leave you only 199 to answer. Phew. At least it will be good practice for when we become famous authors and have to sign books.

I hope you are doing okay.

Love,
Tara★

Date: February 11 5:10:38 PM
From: Eliz812
Subj: A Big Surprise
To: TSTARR

Dear Tara★,

I hardly know what to write first. I'm kind of excited about something that happened today. But I think I have to start by talking about something you said in your letter, something that made so much sense.

Remember when I told you I don't understand why we're so upset about Dad's death? Since he hasn't acted like a father or a husband for a long time? Well, you gave me the answer in your letter. You said Mom must still have loved Dad. Now that I think about it, I still loved him too. I just didn't want to admit it. I mean, what does it say about me that I loved someone who I also wished were dead? Someone who did horrible things to Mom and Emma and me? But of course I still loved him. My father. He was my father. Just realizing that makes me feel better. Not great. But better. Thank you.

Here's what happened today. Howie picked me up this morning and as we were walking to Susie's, I was thinking about asking him to our school's Valentine's Day dance (yes, there is one; it's tomorrow night). I liked your idea that I should be the one to do the asking. Anyway, I was just about to say something when <u>he</u> asked <u>me</u> to the dance! We're going as friends, not boyfriend and girlfriend, and I am looking forward to it. I don't have anything very Valentine-y to wear, but that's okay. Howie doesn't either. We're just going to wear nice-ish school clothes. (By the way, I like the sound of your fuzzy pink sweater. I think that is a great thing to wear to a Valentine's dance.)

Mom and I are still working on the notes. I think maybe we have written about ⅓ of them. (Thank you for saying we don't have to write to you, but you know we will anyway.)

Emma has had three tantrum-free days (not in a row). But she is sucking her thumb MUCH more than usual. Mom says not to worry, that it will pass.

I rethought the D on the social studies assignment and asked the teacher if I could do it over. She said she was wondering when I would ask. She gave me until next Wednesday for the do-over.

Susie asked me to come over for dinner tonight. We are going to have a girls-only evening, since the rest of her family is doing something with Matt's kindergarten class.

Love,
Elizabeth

Date: February 13 6:53:29 PM
From: TSTARR
Subj: You Gotta Have Heart!!!!
To: Eliz812

Dear Elizabeth,
It was so good to get your last e-mail.

I've been so worried about you and this was the first e since your father died that has sounded like . . . you. (I do remember what Barb said about all of the stages you and your mom and Emma will have to go through . . . but I really want you to be happy again.)

You know that I know how difficult your father could be. But — I remember how proud he used to be about your poetry . . . and how he smiled when you won the fourth-grade essay contest. And I understand why you still loved him.

As for the news about your Valentine's Day dance, that was soooooooo terrific. . . . I only wish I could have been there to help you pick out your outfit and accessories. (Even though you would have said, "Oh, Tara, you know I wouldn't be comfortable wearing something like that." And then you would have dressed your own comfortable way.) I wish you had e-mailed me immediately with a report . . . but I know you don't do that. Sometimes you drive me crazy. I NEED to know all about the dance . . . what you wore . . . what Howie wore. (Did he wear the cuff links you gave him?) Did you get or give flowers? Did you dance? Do you two have a "song"? (I know . . . you're just friends.)

Now for a report about my Valentine's Day dance.

It was wonderful!!!!!!!!!

The only problem was that after we slow danced, some of my fluffy pink sweater shed on Phil's T-shirt. I have to remember that sometimes things are on super-sale for a reason!!!!!!!

Hannah was there with her new boyfriend, Bob. (I think it's sooooo cool that his name is a palindrome too!!!!!)

The big news is that at the dance, Phil put a pulltop from a soda can on my finger and asked me to be his girlfriend . . . and I said, "Yes." I'm wearing the pulltop on a chain around my neck.

Phil's mom picked us up after the dance and drove us all home — Phil, me, and the palindromers, Hannah and Bob. At my door, Phil gave me a little kiss, but since everyone was sitting in the car, watching, it was a very little kiss.

Ooops . . . gotta get off the computer and go check on Scarlett, who is screaming her little lungs out. (My parents have gone out on a "date," their first since Scarlett was born.)

Love,
Tara★

Date: February 14 5:34:51 PM
From: Eliz812
Subj: Happy Valentine's Day!!!
To: TSTARR

Dear Tara★,

See? I'm writing to you a LITTLE sooner than I ordinarily would, to say happy Valentine's Day, since today is the actual day.

I'm SO glad you had such a good time at the dance.
So . . . you and Phil are now girlfriend and boyfriend.
That is extremely cool. Howie and I had a great time
too, although we are still just friends. What did we
wear? I wore my good black jeans and a pink-and-
blue-striped sweater (once again, thank you, Value
Town). At least I managed a little pink in the outfit.
Howie also wore jeans, but they were regular blue

ones, and a rugby shirt. He didn't wear the cuff links because no one got very dressed up for the dance.

For some reason, I was thinking about Dad a lot during the dance. Maybe because three of the chaperones were kids' fathers. At first I thought, wouldn't it be great if my dad were here too? Then I thought — which dad? The one who wasn't around much even when he <u>was</u> around? The drunk dad? It was sad because it was so confusing. I almost cried. Then Howie asked me to dance. I stepped on his feet a lot, which was funny until I started to watch Beth Coburn dancing with her father. And I realized I would never be able to dance with Dad.

Mom and I had a good talk yesterday. Emma was over at Matt's, and Mom and I were working on the notes again. I looked up from one and saw Mom crying, and then I started to cry too, and all of a sudden we were just hugging and crying for the longest time. Finally I told Mom that I couldn't help thinking about all the times I said I wished Dad were dead, or that we were better off without him in our lives. Mom said what you said, Tara. That of course wishing doesn't make things happen. But then she said she thought she might call Mrs. Jackson to see if she can recommend a therapist for kids. I wouldn't mind talking to somebody. Mom is great, you are great, but it would be good to talk to someone who didn't know Dad.

After Mom and I finished crying, we abandoned the notes for a while. We talked about Dad, about the accident, the funeral, you and Luke. I told her I would never, ever, ever forget the sight of the coffin being lowered into the ground. I won't.

I feel like my life is a book and a section of it has just ended. I'm a little afraid to turn the page to find out what the next section is titled. But not too afraid. I guess I'll be able to turn it knowing that you and Barb and Luke and Howie and Susie and my mom and Emma and so many other people are standing with me. I don't see how anything bad could be written on that page with all of you there to read it with me.

More later.

Love,
Elizabeth

Date: February 14 10:03:27 PM
From: TSTARR
Subj: Life: A Novel Approach
To: Eliz812

Thinking about life as a book is really great. . . . You know what I like best?!?! We'll always be characters in each other's "books" . . . and even when there are "bad" things written on our "pages," we'll always be there, as real people, to help each other out.

Have I told you lately that I'm glad we are friends?

Love,
Tara★

SHEPHERD MIDDLE SCHOOL LIBRARY
701 E. McKinley Road
Ottawa, IL 61350
815-434-7925

500327   12/09

DEMCO